Goldilocks & the Three Bear Brothers
-Third Edition-

By Pebbles Lacasse

From the Naughty Goldie Series

Originally featured as Book 2 in
LaSasha Flame's
Torrid Tales: Fairy Tales Retold Collection

Copyright

Third Edition
Published by Pebbles Lacasse
Cover design by Pebbles Lacasse
Cover model J. M.
Edited by Jody Freeman – Off the Shelf Editing

SPECIAL MESSAGE FROM THE AUTHOR

Hello, Playmates!

The original *Goldilocks and the Three Bears* fairy tale is a cute story we all heard as children. It's about a girl who stumbles upon the home of a family of bears. She tests out the belongings of each bear to figure out which she most prefers.

I wrote this book with very much the same idea, with a wickedly sexy twist. My erotic version is not only about the sexual aspect of meeting a family of three brothers in the forest—these human men offer her more than just porridge and a place to rest her head.

The reason I chose this particular fairy tale is a simple one: what erotic romance writer wouldn't want to start with the premise of a beautiful woman and three hot woodsmen? As soon as Goldilocks popped into my head, I knew it had to be mine. I immediately put everything else aside and ran with it.

I hope you enjoy my version of *Goldilocks and the Three Bears*. At the end of the book is a sneak peek of the first few chapters of **Goldilocks and the Three Bear Brothers: Trifecta, book two**, available now on Amazon. You'll also find more books I've written and social media links so you can keep up with me.

Much love,
Pebbles Lacasse

CHAPTER ONE

The summer has been long, or at least it seems so. I've been living with my parents for the past three months and I can't wait to head back to the dorms in the big city. I'll be leaving home for the final time in three days. After this semester, I'll have extra credits toward my degree and will begin my life as an independent adult. I won't lie, it scares me a bit.

My parents are truly wonderful, but overbearing. I'm twenty-three and they still want to know where I'm going, what I'll be doing, and who I'm going to be doing it with. When it comes to dating, the guy has to be parent approved. I couldn't count how many times I've heard the fifteen-minute lecture on how bad boys never change and they'll give good girls terrible reputations. I think they're just worried about how their friends will judge them on their parenting if I date an unsuitable.

I recently ended it with a guy I'd dated for just over a year. His name was Jeff and he was parent approved. He's studying to become a mortgage lawyer and he bored the hell out of me! The guy never wanted to go anywhere that didn't involve his parents tagging along, and he only ever took me to places that were so snooze-inducing I could barely keep my eyes open. The man even made me yawn in bed. I don't think I ever had an orgasm that I didn't give myself.

Before Jeff there was Sebastian, also parent approved. He too bored me. He could make me cum, but he enjoyed missionary position and never veered from it, and always had a lame excuse as to why he didn't want to try a different position. We dated for about six months, but I ended it when I moved away to university. I told him a long-distance relationship would simply be too difficult. He cried. I was relieved to be rid of him but pretended I wasn't so I wouldn't hurt him even more.

Before him was Cody, a good boy from our town. He was also stamped for parental approval. We dated for two years and ended the summer before I became a high school senior. We had sex a few times and it was good but short. He didn't enjoy going down on me and that was frustrating. He loved getting blowjobs though. It didn't take long for me to insist it be tit-for-tat. If he didn't eat my pussy, I wouldn't suck his prick.

He fucked hard with his big cock, but he couldn't last more than two minutes at best.

All I've ever wanted is to find a decent guy who knows how to have excellent sex that benefits me as well as him. I don't think it's too much to ask. I want someone who loves to make me cum with their mouth, fucks like the devil himself, and has an endless desire to pleasure me with new and exciting sexual adventures. Maybe I can find a bad boy that knows how to thrill me if I stop dating the good boys.

My room looks exactly the same as it did before I moved away for school. The pictures of my childhood friends still frame the old mirror I spent hours upon hours staring into, trying to make myself look different from who I am. High school and those awful teenage mood-swings were unbearable, but overall the experience was enjoyable.

I choose my senior high school yearbook from the long rows of books on my wall-to-wall shelf. I want to reminisce about the good days when life was easier, but at the time, I thought it was so hard. If I only knew back then how tough it could get, I'd have made it a point to enjoy my teens more.

When I toss it on the bed, the book falls open to the page I've masturbated to many times. Staring back at me is an all too familiar half-page photo of the hottest boy in high school. His wavy chestnut hair and piercing blue eyes make my heart skip a beat. My eyes trace the strong jaw framing the plump, inviting lips, wishing I could taste them. Bash Bear. Yes, it's a funny name for such a ruggedly handsome man. I would never have dated him—he wasn't parent approved. In fact, my parents forbid me to spend time with any of the Bear brothers.

All three still reside in the cottage that sits directly between the house I grew up in, where my parents still reside, and the closest town. I could best describe the area as a thick forest with many back trails we use for dirt bikes, ATVs, snowmobiles, and hiking. There's only one road leading in to town and it's a single lane dirt road that winds around the Bear property.

While driving by, I'd always look through the trees hoping to see one of those hunky guys but rarely did. The only brother I'd see regularly was Bash, the youngest of the three. He took the same school bus as me. They all have wide shoulders, stand quite tall, and are as strong as bulls.

If I missed the bus, I'd walk the trail that leads through the corner of the Bear brothers' fifteen-hundred-acre private property. It's the fastest way to get to town, even though it zigzags the whole way. Sometimes I would see one of them cutting down a tree or hunting with a bow and arrow, but they would only watch me. Never did they try to strike up a conversation. Even if they had, I was too shy to talk to them. I would have likely just kept walking.

Bash would talk to me once in a while in the morning on the bus. He and I were the only two students to board for the next eight minutes when we'd arrived at Stacey's pick-up spot. She always talked to Bash. She was desperately in love with him. He didn't show her much interest other than friendship. That didn't stop her from making a fool of herself by so obviously swooning over him.

I slam my yearbook shut and slip it back in its spot on the shelf. I'm not a silly high school girl with a crush anymore. I'm an adult woman and I can do whatever I'd like. My body is mine to do with as I please, and it's not up for debate with my parents anymore.

My heart pounds as I strip off my clothes and step into the shower. I'm going to go walking in the woods after I'm clean and smell better. Maybe I'll find one of the Bear brothers, the hunky bad boys my parents forbid me to talk to. If I fuck one of them, who will know? Nobody. It'll be our secret, as if it never happened.

They aren't known for boasting about their sexual conquests; in fact, they've denied being with some women who have told tales of incredible sexual romps that only happen in dirty magazines or pornos. Sex that good isn't real life.

I slip on a white summer dress, omitting the panties. I forgo a bra since my round breasts are perky and firm. Besides, the light material allows for my nipples to form stiff peaks that will draw any hot-blooded man's attention. I glide my hands down my small waist, resting them on my full hips. Yes, I look good in this. I usually wear heels with this dress even though I'm plenty tall enough without them. Today, I'll wear the proper foot attire since I'll be hiking.

After quickly drying my long blonde hair, I pull it up into a high ponytail. Makeup isn't something I'm all that skilled at applying. Whenever I try to outline my sky-blue eyes with a pencil, I end up looking like I have two black eyes, so I'll skip it, as usual. A spritz of perfume and I'm ready for an afternoon of forbidden lust, if I'm lucky enough to run into a Bear.

After another quick check from head to toe in the mirror, I go to the bathroom to pee and wash my hands. While the warm water runs over my fingers, I stare at myself in the mirror. "You've always been a good girl. Today, you're a dirty little whore. You are a strong, independent woman who needs a bad boy to fuck her into a coma." I take a deep breath and dry my hands before heading to the kitchen.

"Mom, I'm heading out for a walk."

"Wait, where are you going?" she asks as I quickly walk past her.

"Just for a walk. I want to soak up as much of this nature as I can before heading back to school."

The city is so hustle and bustle. She knows I enjoy the solitude of the vast forest. I'm going to miss the smell of the moss and the dark quietness from the thick canopy of trees.

She smiles. "I wish you didn't have to return to school but it's what's best for you."

Dad walks into the kitchen from outside, carrying an empty mug. He drinks his first coffee on the porch while reading the newspaper. Morning is his quiet time, as he calls it. He's wearing a scowl likely brought on by the political section. "Don't be walking on the Bear property. Those boys can't be trusted. You know all about their bad reputation."

"Dad, I'm sure they won't care if I walk the paths that lead through their property. They're not as bad as you think they are."

"Yes, they are! The middle boy—" Dad starts.

"Mack."

"I don't care what his name is. He's been arrested for despicable offences that we won't talk about."

"You mean drunk and nude in public, right?" My giggling has him pursing his lips.

"Just stay away from those boys, Goldilocks," Mom says, hoping my father will leave it at that.

"Mom, Dad, I don't plan on being home until late. I have my whistle in case I see a real bear that might actually harm me."

I quickly slip on my hiking boots and rush out the door. I can hear them talking to each other, but I pay no attention and head across the yard toward the path that will lead me to a possible Bear sighting. My heart thumps rapidly in my chest as I near the barely-readable wooden sign posted on the tree stating the property is private, no trespassing. It's there only for the purpose of non-locals who think its okay to hunt wherever they want without the owner's permission.

My heart sinks after about twenty minutes of walking and seeing not a single soul. I'm not a slut, but today, I want to be treated like one. I've allotted myself this one day to be bad, and dammit, if I have to go knocking on their door to ask for a cup of sugar, that's exactly what I'll do. Will I have the courage to ask for sex? I doubt it.

I hear a chainsaw rev up not too far from me, halting me mid-step. A warm shiver runs down my spine that I welcome. This is scary, thrilling, and dangerous. Well, maybe not so dangerous.

I step off the path and head toward the sound. There he is, Patch. He's wearing a long-sleeved black and white button-up plaid shirt, but the buttons aren't fastened, allowing it to flow as he moves, showing off his tanned chest. His heavy gloves grip the thunderous tool as it easily slices through the log like a hot knife through cold butter. His muscles glisten with sweat.

The chainsaw idles as he kicks the freshly cut log out of his way using the sole of his heavy black boot. The saw revs up again as his strong thighs flex to steady his body, allowing him to lift the heavy, vibrating machine. He lowers it onto the tree's stump, cutting off another chunk of firewood. It idles once again after that piece falls.

He suddenly turns, locking his brown eyes on me. My fear has me frozen in place. Patch is the oldest of the brothers and the one who is known to have a mean streak. He's never hit a woman, but he sure can clean the floor with a husky man when the need arises.

Patch turns his body to face me, setting the saw on the thick, moss-covered ground. With his eyes assessing me, he slowly removes his gloves, dropping them beside the quiet saw. The breeze feels hotter than it had only a few seconds ago. Maybe it's just me, but the temperature seems to have risen ten degrees.

"Hello, Goldilocks. What brings you out this way? You lost?" His voice is so deep that it stirs the carnal desire I've had locked away inside me for far too long.

I clear my throat, realizing how suddenly dry it is. "No, I'm not lost."

"I thought you were away at school," he says as he opens his jug, taking a long swig of what I assume to be water.

"I've been home for the summer, but I'll be heading back soon."

"Thirsty?" he asks, waving the jug in my direction.

I nod and start walking toward him. It's not a lie, I'm absolutely parched and regretting not taking a bottle of water with me. It's a long walk. What was I thinking? He hands me the jug. I've never stood this close to Patch before and it's been years since I've even set eyes on him. He's more handsome than I remember him to be.

I take a large mouthful and swallow, suddenly realizing it isn't water. Whatever it is, it burns my throat. I grimace and cough, feeling like an idiot.

Patch snickers, taking the jug back when I hold it out to him. "Moonshine. I make it myself. Do you like it?"

I cough again. "It … burns."

He laughs and takes a long swig before putting the cap back on and sitting it on the ground next to his gloves.

"What brings you out this way?"

I suddenly wish I had taken a larger gulp of the poison in his bottle. "Um, I don't know. I suppose I'm just out for a walk in the forest."

"Is that so? You're definitely not a little girl who missed her school bus and needs to cut through my property." His eyes scan my body in an obvious manner. "So, what other reason could you have for trespassing?"

He steps closer to me, his eyes glaring down into mine. I'm shivering despite the heat. I take a deep breath and let it out slowly, hoping to regain some composure.

"No, I'm not a little girl anymore."

His eyes slowly look down to my breasts and back up. "You grew into yourself nicely. So tell me, why are you here, sexy woman?"

I simply shrug and look down, unable to find the words to explain. My heart thumps so loudly in my ears. All I can hear are the leaves rustling in the trees, yet everything he says sounds crystal clear. My eyes land on his strong abs. No matter how hard I try to look away, I can't seem to make it happen.

"You're a good girl, Goldilocks. I'm definitely not good. What the hell do you want with me?"

As if overcome by the spirit of a slut, I reply with, "I am not as innocent as everyone thinks. Maybe I want to be bad for once in my life. I've always done the right thing, said the right thing, and been the best I can be. I don't want to be that perfect little girl today."

Patch takes two quick steps toward me, grasping the back of my neck with one hand, wrapping the other around my back, pulling me against him until my breasts press firmly to his wide chest. I can smell the salt on his sweaty skin and feel his raging body heat.

"Are you a virgin?" he whispers.

I shake my head. "I'm not a virgin, but my experience is limited."

"What does that mean? Has your pussy ever been fucked hard?" His thin lips are so close that the vibration from his voice can be felt on my lips.

"I've been fucked hard, just not good."

"I can fuck you really good."

His mouth presses to mine, spreading my lips with his. He explores my entire mouth with his moonshine flavored tongue. It tastes better this way. His flesh burns through the thin fabric of my dress. He grabs my ass, pinching a whole cheek firmly in his grip. The bulge in his tight, torn jeans digs into my belly and grows larger by the second. In a flash he spins me, grabbing my throat and right breast to hold me against him while his lips rest just behind my left ear.

I whimper when his deep voice rattles me. "Tell me you want me to fuck you hard and fast, Goldilocks."

"I … I want you to fuck me hard and fast," I manage to mutter with an obvious stutter. I'm terrified and thrilled at the same time, much like sitting on a rollercoaster and expecting one hell of a ride.

Patch releases my breast but continues his grip on my throat. He steps back, yanking my dress up to expose my ass. "Surprise, surprise! No panties. Perhaps you're not as innocent as everyone thinks."

He slides his hand around to the back of my neck, using that advantage to bend me forward. He's holding my hip with the other hand so I can't move away from him. Once my ass is exposed and vulnerable, he releases my neck, dragging his fingertips along my spine, continuing down the crease between my ass cheeks until he reaches my slippery pussy. He smears my arousal up and down the folds of my pussy, purposely avoiding my twitching clitoris.

Holy fuck! This is definitely starting to be a tale I could send to one of those magazines.

I hear his zipper pull down. The thought of him standing behind me with his hard-on in his hand excites me even more. Here we are, surrounded by the forest, nearly nude and about to fuck beneath the silent canopy of tall trees. I've never even had sex outside of a bedroom, let alone outdoors.

His legs part and his boots rest on either side of mine. The tip of his prick lines up to the opening of my eager pussy. My heart is pounding furiously behind my ribs. He rubs the thick head up and down my slick lips. With one long, slow push forward, he buries himself deep into me. I cry out but love the stretch. His prick is a nice size; not too big and definitely not small.

"You fit nice, little girl," he grumbles. "Are you ready?"

"Will you fuck me hard?"

"I sure as fuck will."

"Then yes, I'm ready."

His huge hands grab my waist, nearly surrounding it. He jerks me back while slamming his hips forward. I nearly lose my footing. He snickers but immediately does it again. This time, I'm prepared for it.

Oh yes, this is going to be amazing! He rams me again but doesn't pause this time. His cock fills me, relentlessly pounding into me. I've never been fucked this viciously, nor this fast. My head is spinning.

My moans and the sound of our bodies slapping together ricochet from tree to tree. It takes all the strength I have to keep my legs from collapsing. I'm coming already! He's only pounded into me a dozen times and I'm already crying out. My body freezes in a state of awe, reveling in the glory of my first orgasm from being fucked incredibly hard and fast by a Bear.

"Yes!" In my experience, it'll be over soon. "Please don't stop! Fuck me! Fuck…"

My words stick in my throat when I'm overwhelmed by another body tightening climax. My knees buckle but I don't fall. Patch is hanging onto my waist so tightly that I seem to be dangling off his cock.

I am a vessel for him to fuck, a piece of ass willingly given to him to use as he will.

"You're a fucking slut, aren't you? You're not a good little girl. You're a dirty little whore," he growls.

"Yes … I'm a … fucking … whore!" Another raging orgasm tears through me even more violently than the first two. My legs have turned into cooked spaghetti noodles. It's useless to try to stand; I know they can't sustain my weight.

Patch's solid cock slips from my body. He spins me to face him. He grabs my ass in one hand and the back of my head in the other. His lips press to mine while he walks me backward toward a tree.

He pulls my dress up and over my head and tosses it over a branch. Instinct is to cover my nakedness, but I clutch my hands into fists to fight that urge. His menacing eyes ogle my bare breasts and naked mound.

"I've often wondered what you look like under your clothes, after you were grown, of course. You're just as fucking hot as I'd imagined, probably more so. Goldilocks, turn around and bend over that tree trunk. You'd better hang on because I'm going to fuck the hell out of your cunt."

I smile while biting my bottom lip. If it's anything like how he's been fucking me, I want more of it, lots more. Not to seem too eager, I think I'll take my time getting into position. I let my eyes sink down to his chest and further, past his ripped abs. His hand is gripping his stiff prick. I want it back inside of me. I turn, placing my hands on the bark of the tree, and bending slightly while turning my face to look at his. I see him lick his bottom lip as his eyes lock on my behind.

"I would love to fuck that sweet ass of yours," he comments.

I quickly straighten up and spin around. My mood instantly shifts from whore-mode to terrified virgin. "I've never … I mean … you're not going to…"

He snickers. "I'm not going to shove my cock in your ass, if that's what you're asking. I don't do anything without permission. Judging by the look on your face, I'm assuming I don't have your permission."

"No, I've never actually done that."

"Mack would be the best one of us three to de-virgin your asshole. If you'd be interested in trying that, I'm sure he'd oblige you. His cock is thinner than mine. He's gentle despite his rough appearance. He loves to eat pussy but ass is his favorite hole to fuck."

"I'd be interested in trying. I've heard my girlfriends talk about anal but my boyfriends would never try it. They said it was dirty and gross." I can't help but roll my eyes and giggle nervously.

"Okay, let's find him, shall we?"

He pulls his cell phone from his back pocket and taps it. He holds it screen up, touching the speaker icon. I hear it ring.

CHAPTER TWO

A man speaks with a voice similar to Patch's. "What the fuck do you want?"

"Hey, what are you up to?" Patch asks.

"Why? Do you miss me?"

"I don't miss your ugly fucking mug. I'm standing before a gorgeous and naked Goldilocks."

"Like fuck you are! No way is that fine piece of ass coming anywhere near the likes of you. She'd come for my fat tongue long before your limp cock." I hear the phone click. "Fucker hung up!"

Patch presses some numbers before holding the phone flat again.

"What the fuck, man?" Mack yells after answering the call.

Patch tells me, "Say hello, Goldilocks."

"Hello Mack," I say toward the phone. My hand instinctively covers my mouth, hoping I won't burst out laughing.

"Are you fucking with me? Is that really Goldilocks?"

"Yeah, in the flesh and nothing else. She just rode my pole."

"Fuck off! No way! Who is that?"

"Goldilocks! I'm not fucking lying to you. She has a proposition for you."

"I won't believe you until you take a picture of her and send it to me."

I shake my head when Patch holds up his phone. He tells me, "Cover your face if you prefer."

With my hand over my eyes, he snaps a shot. A few seconds later I hear the sound of the photo being sent. I'm suddenly very self-conscious.

"Holy fuck! You weren't bullshitting me! That's really her!"

"Yeah, fucker, that's what I've been trying to tell you."

"Goddamn, she's fucking hot! Okay, so what's this proposition you were talking about?"

"I don't think you really want to know. Maybe I'll just keep her to myself."

"Patch, don't tease me like this, man!"

"Well, the lovely Goldilocks has never had the pleasure of having a cock in her ass, and she'd like to experience it. I told her you were the best."

"Well, I am the best," he boasts. I hear Mack clear his throat. "Are you fucking with me?"

"No, I'm not. So, what do you say? Would you kindly fuck this gorgeous woman's virgin ass before she heads back to school in a few days?"

"It'd be my pleasure! Well, hers too, of course. Where are you?"

"We're about a hundred feet north of where Bash wiped out on the dirt bike and busted his arm."

"Which arm?"

They're both chuckling as if it's hilarious that he's broken more than just one of his limbs. I vaguely recall him starting his junior year of high school with a cast on his left arm.

"His ulna, not his humerus. He broke that at Dog's Creek."

"Oh yeah! That was a hell of a wipe out!" Mack laughs. "I can be there in about ten minutes unless you'd rather meet at the house."

"I'll bring her home with me," Patch replies while handing my dress to me. His eyes study my curves before it slips over my head. He stuffs his hard prick back into his jeans.

"Aren't you going to finish?"

"Not right now," he replies.

"I'm nervous." I don't know why I just confessed that to him.

"Goldilocks, there's nothing to fear. Mack will be very gentle. I'll be there to make sure of it."

"You're going to be there … like, watching us?"

"Were you thinking you and I were done? Woman, I haven't fucked you hard enough yet and definitely not long enough. After he's done with you, you're going to finish me off."

I shake my head. "I don't know about that. I'll probably be exhausted by then."

He says, "I doubt it. You'll want more. Whores always want more." My pussy clenches.

We start walking back to the house after he collects his chainsaw and half-empty jug of moonshine. I lead the way. I'm sure he's watching my ass move beneath my dress. To make things more fun, I pinch the back hem of my dress and lift it, exposing my ass.

"You're a fucking tease, aren't you? I should drop this shit and finish us both off."

"So, why don't you?" I taunt him with a sweet innocence that doesn't suit the situation.

He laughs. "Because, little slut, I'm going to make you wait."

"I thought I was a whore. First I'm a slut, then I'm a whore. I wish you'd make up your mind." I tease partly to make conversation so my anxiety doesn't overwhelm me, thus beckoning me to change my mind.

"Do you have a preference?"

I laugh. "No, I'm just making fun of your unoriginal choices of degrading titles."

"I was only asking out of kindness. I'll call you whatever I damn well please. You said you wanted to be bad today, so be bad, really fucking bad. Be a whore, a slut who needs cocks, lots of cocks. Beg to be filled in every hole like a dirty slut who can't get enough."

I turn and look him in the eye. "Please tell me you don't think I'm actually slutty, aside from today, of course."

He stops walking so he won't slam into me. "I know you're a good girl, but even good girls have needs that should be fulfilled. I don't think anybody has given you the attention you deserve. Today, you can be as bad as you want. Nobody is judging you. You can act like a total cum-guzzling whore if you want to. It wouldn't be the first time a good girl begged us to let her be bad. You just happen to be the good girl us brothers have dreamed of getting our hands on but never thought it possible."

"You all have? Even Bash?" I bite my lip nervously, hoping he'll tell me that Bash has spoken favorably of me.

"Goldilocks, Bash has mentioned you on many occasions. I think he'd prefer a relationship with you, but he would settle for a romp." He tilts his head. "You like Bash, don't you?"

"I've always had a crush on Bash. All three of you are gorgeous, each in your own way. Bash ... he's ... different. Yes, I really like Bash."

Before he can say anything else, I turn to continue making my way through the forest with Patch in tow and my dress hiked above my waist, Bash in my thoughts. Just before we come to the clearing where the cottage sits, I drop my dress despite Patch's disapproving groan.

My pace must have slowed because he zips past me. I quickly catch up. We round the house to find Mack sitting on the long porch on a heavy, wooden chair with a beer in his hand, bare feet propped on a wooden stump. He seems darker and more mysterious from being shadowed by the overhanging roof. He's bare-chested and his faded, low-rise jeans have tears in both knees.

"Do you want a beer?" he asks while wearing that same sexy crooked smile that used to make the girls fall at his feet.

"I'd love one," I reply.

"Get me one too," Patch adds before Mack slips into the house.

"What's the matter, your moonshine burning a hole in your gut?"

"Keep mouthing off, slut, and I'll put something in that yap to shut you up," Patch says as he winks. He points to a chair across from the one Mack was sitting in.

I sit and lean back, closing my eyes for a moment to fully appreciate the warmth of the sun on my face. Beneath the canopy of trees is much cooler than here in the clearing. When I open them, Mack is standing in front of me handing me a beer. I take it and smile, noticing that his hair is wet from a recent shower. He smells nice too.

"Thank you." The beer is cold and satisfying as it flows down my throat.

Mack sits back in his chair while Patch walks into the house, the screen door slamming closed behind him. He looks at the peaks my nipples have formed in my dress and licks his lips slowly. His eyes lift to mine as he takes a long swig of his beer. I haven't looked away from him yet.

"So, you want to experience a cock in your ass. Is that right?" He's very blunt.

I fight my habit of playing shy. "I've never tried it, but it comes highly recommended by some of my friends. No one has ever wanted to do that with me."

He grunts, his eyebrows furrowing into a scowl. "You're not the type of girl to have random sex with two men in one day. What's gotten into you, other than my brother's dick I'm assuming?"

I shrug and clear my throat to eradicate the puff of cotton that seems to be looming. "I feel as though

I've missed out on so much of what life has to offer. People are always telling me about their wild sexual experiences in college, but I don't have anything to boast about. The men I've been with have been rather boring."

"So, you came to visit my brother?"

"Not specifically." I take a long drink of beer, nearly finishing it. I elaborate when he doesn't say anything. "You boys have always been off limits to me. For years, my parents have been warning me to stay away from all three of you. I've heard some stories through the rumor mill about you guys being hot lays. So, I thought I'd start walking this way and see if I'd run into one of you."

As Patch opens the screen door, he says, "She wants to be very, very bad for only one day. Today. I promised her we would let her be as bad as she wants to be. But this little woman has it in for our baby brother."

"Well, they are closest in age," Mack adds.

I whisper, "Yeah, but he'll never want me after I've had his brothers inside me."

"Is that a joke?" Mack snickers.

"No guy wants a girl who slutted herself out to his brothers. Life doesn't work that way." I set my empty beer bottle down on the chunk of tree they use as a table. "So, are we doing this? If I sit here any longer, I'll either get too drunk to give my consent or lose my nerve and run away, regretting that decision for the rest of my life."

I don't wait for his response. I stand and walk past Patch, then pull the screen door open and walk into their house before either of them even gets to their feet. It's cleaner than I had expected, considering three men live here.

The cabin is made from long logs which give it a rustic appearance, but the furniture is what draws my attention. Everything is made from trees that were plucked from the surrounding acreage and built by hand. Even the bed frame I can see through the open door of one of the bedrooms is made from immature tree trunks. I love this house!

I'm startled when a thick hand slides into mine. Mack is looking back at me with eyes more tender than I have ever known them to be while leading me toward a bedroom. He guides me into a large bedroom.

Mack lifts my chin and smiles at me. He brushes a stray lock of hair from my cheek, tucking it gently behind my ear. My knees are shaking and I'm taking deep breaths to help me remain calm.

"I'll be gentle with you, especially since this is your first time. I don't want to hurt you. You'll need to tell me if you're in pain or if you want me to stop for any reason. At first, it'll feel uncomfortable. Stay calm and relaxed, I'll move slowly. As your ass stretches, you'll start to enjoy it more and more."

"Trust me, if I don't like it, I'll definitely speak up," I assure him.

His lips press to mine just once. "Take off your dress."

I wish I had drunk another beer. I came here to get fucked in the ass and that's what I'm going to do. Off goes my dress. I stand before him completely nude while he casually undresses, not giving my body so much as a glance. Mack pulls open a dresser drawer and takes a small bottle out before pushing it closed. He ushers me to the bed and asks me to lie on my back. I do as he asks.

"Do you enjoy receiving oral sex?" he whispers seductively.

"Of course. It feels good, after all."

"Did my brother cum inside you?"

"No, he didn't finish."

He touches both of my knees gently while looking at my eyes. The heat from his hands radiates across my skin, warming my entire body. He lowers his face to my mound and begins lapping at my clitoris. It isn't long before I'm moaning and humping up to meet each stroke of his tongue. Mack teases my ass with a fingertip, and I clench instinctually.

"You have to relax," he instructs as his finger continues to taunt my asshole.

To distract me, he sucks my clitoris painfully hard and I scream. My hands grab wads of his long, wet hair, ready to yank him off me if he does it again. I'm startled to realize that his finger is in my ass, wiggling and cautiously pulling at it. Stranger yet, my clit is twitching wildly because of it.

I concentrate on relaxing while enjoying his lips and tongue. He isn't working my clit enough to bring me to orgasm, but I don't think that's his intention at this point in time. Soon, he has two digits inside my tight hole, both pulling to stretch it wide enough to compensate his cock's girth.

I took a quick gander at his prick while he was getting undressed. Patch didn't lie when he said Mack's cock is smaller than his. It's longer, but thinner. He isn't any larger than what's evacuated my body, therefore I'm not as afraid to have him inside my ass as I would be if he were larger.

He sucks my swelling clit until it's thick and hard, ready to erupt my body into a vicious orgasm. Much to my dismay, he stops and flips me onto my belly, lifting my ass up by my hips until I'm on my knees and shoving a pillow beneath me.

He slides up behind me, kneeling behind me. He presses the head of his slippery cock against my well lubricated asshole. More cold liquid drips onto my flesh as he slowly begins to fill me, stopping each time I tense and patiently waiting for me to relax before continuing.

It isn't long before he's completely buried deep inside my asshole with his pelvis pressing against my ass cheeks. I feel so full, so dirty, so slutty! This is taboo; very raunchy and nasty. I love the mental aspect of it as much as the sensation of being full.

Each time he pulls back, I feel relief. When he pushes back in, that changes the sensation to one that's foreign to me, but I like it very much. My thoughts keep drifting away from reality. My focus is on the pleasure I feel each time his prick glides along my inner walls. It's as if he rubs nerves I didn't know existed, each one shooting tiny tickles directly into in my clit. What a thrill this is!

Mack asks me to lie face down with a pillow under my hips, my legs slightly spread. His thighs are straddling my butt cheeks with his feet draped over the back of my knees, pinning them down. His ass lifts and lowers, drilling into me with an easy rhythmic motion that has me moaning with each deep penetration.

He pulls the elastic band from my ponytail, setting my hair free. His fingers weave into it, grasping it firmly. The heat of his breath on my cheek and the weight of his chest on my back create a scenario of being under his control. I like it. I like feeling as if he can do whatever he wants to me and I am defenseless to do anything about it. I like it because I know I can yell for him to get off of me and he will. I feel safe in my vulnerability, even though I don't know Mack all that well.

His reputation around town isn't a good one. He's been described as a scruffy, feisty guy with strange perversions and a bad attitude. None of which describes the man making love to my ass. Mack is freshly showered, drizzled with a sweet, manly cologne and he's more tender than any lover has ever been with me. His touch is strong but velvety; loving, I'd be willing to say.

Mack's hand slips beneath my tummy and down toward my clit. The instant his fingertips glide over my button, I whimper and grind my hips down onto them. His fingers swirl and stroke my swollen nub, urging me closer and closer to the edge. I don't want to cum. If I do, this will end, and I dread that. I've only ever been able to cum once during play because my clit becomes too painfully sensitive to touch.

My hips lift, desperate to evade his fingers but my efforts are forted. His prick fucks faster, really working my asshole and forcing my pussy down onto his fingers. I can't hold my climax back any longer.

Every muscle starting at my belly button exploding outward begins to tighten until I am rigid and unmoving. My lungs fill and hold. It feels like a balloon is filling with heat inside of me, bloating my entire vagina from within my depths. It's going to burst! I've never had this sensation hold for so long. Orgasms are usually so quick to end, but not this time.

I'm panting short breaths, each one laced with increasingly loud moans until a powerful scream blasts from my core. I'm coming harder and more gloriously than I ever have in my entire life! I seem to be stuck at the height of climax for a long time. Suddenly, something enters my sloppy wet pussy and begins waving. Fingers ... they must be Patch's fingers. I don't care who's they are! Just don't stop! Don't ever stop!

With a violent shutter, my orgasm peaks. Only my body exists, nothing else, no one else. Each part of my pussy is twitching, pushing, and gripping with spasms.

Hot! Hot and wet! So wet! Sloshing wet! I am writhing beneath this strong man whose weight is pinning me to the bed. I couldn't get him off me if I tried, not that I want that to happen. I feel light now, as if I'm floating up to the heavens and taking him with me.

His fingers are still twiddling my aching clit, but it doesn't at all hurt. I want him to make me cum again, just like the last time. I need it! I need him to keep going! The fingers are still filling me, stretching my tight pussy and I love the ache they bring.

"Oh, yes! Fuck my ass! Oh, please, make me cum again. Please!" I'm pleading like a desperate whore.

I've never felt anything as completely overwhelming as this. I need to cum again to prove to my mind that it was indeed real and magnificent. The whole experience feels like a glorious dream, a dream that continues to this very moment.

I'm going to cum again! Never has my clit cum again so soon post-orgasm. The fingers fuck me slowly while Mack drills his prick into my ass with a quick, steady pace. Something cold is pressed against my clit. It's vibrating! I don't own a vibrator and have never experienced one. Holy shit!

I'm immediately jerking, thrusting my hips, and wail, sounding like a wild animal in the throes of a mighty battle. I jerk before coming to a statue-like stillness. I'm thrown into a whole-body engulfing, mind-dazing euphoria. I don't know what happens during the next few seconds. My muscles jerk, pulling me back from the distant existence I've drifted off to. I'm exhausted. Every inch of my skin is tingling.

Mack pulls out of my ass as the fingers leave my pussy. He rolls off me, kisses my cheek gently, and gets off the bed. I hear his bare feet slap the floor as he leaves me to the quietness of my mind. All I can hear are my satisfactory whimpers and the pounding of my overworked heart.

CHAPTER THREE

I hear a scuffling of shoes on the floor and it startles me. I thought I was alone. Mack left the room so who is here with me? It must be Patch getting ready to finish fucking me like he said he would do after Mack had his way with me.

"Patch, have you been here the whole time?" I ask with a fatigued voice.

"No and I hope you're not disappointed, but I'm not Patch."

I quickly flip over and sit up, pulling the sheet with me to cover myself. Bash is leaning against the doorframe with his hands in his pants pockets and a quirky grin on his face.

"How long have you been standing there? Were those your fingers in me?"

He nods. "Yes, those were mine. I came home and Patch told me you were in here with Mack trying anal for the first time. I had to come see if he was bullshitting me. When I saw that it was you, I wanted you to have the best first anal sex experience possible. So, I helped out. I hope you don't mind."

"Um, no, I suppose I don't. I'm sorry you had to see me like that." I pause, shaking my head rapidly. He looks at me strangely. "I'm sorry, I don't know what I'm supposed to say right now."

"Goldie, I like you. I've always liked you."

He walks over and sits beside me on the bed. I'm extremely uncomfortable because I'm nude beneath this sheet and suddenly emotionally vulnerable, regretting my decision to fuck his brothers. Does he think I'm a whore now and wants nothing to do with me? I pull the sheet tighter over my chest, dreading that thought. If he were disgusted with me, he wouldn't be sitting on the bed with me after having fingered me into one of the best climaxes of my life. It makes no sense, him saying he likes me after having just watched me get my ass pounded by Mack.

He takes my hand in his. "I respect you, always have. You're a nice girl with a solid head on your shoulders. You know what you want in life and you aren't afraid to go after it, no matter what anyone tells you. To be completely honest, you intimidate the hell out of me."

"I am? You really think I ... do I?"

He snickers. "Yes, you do. You've always been better than me and I like that. To see you here enjoying yourself like this is wonderful. Patch said you had your heart set on experiencing what it's like to be a bad girl by doing some taboo things. I think that's great. Everyone should let their hair down now and then to break up the monotony. Life can be boring, but it doesn't have to be."

"Maybe you did like me in high school, but after what just happened, you aren't going to see me in the same light."

"No, I won't. I'll see you in a better light. It makes me want to know you more."

"Oh, I see. You only want to fuck me now."

"Yes, I do, but there's more to it. I'd like to take you out to dinner, get to know you better."

I smile and ask, "Where did Mack go? He just left without a word."

"He's probably in the shower."

"I'd like to ask him if he came in my ass or not."

"No, he didn't finish," Bash states matter-of-fact.

"What is it with you Bear brothers? Do any of you like to cum or do you all prefer to avoid it?"

"We like coming just fine, thank you. We prefer to make sure the woman is completely satisfied before we take our pleasure."

"So, they're going to come back in here and do me again?"

"Is that such a bad thing?" he asks with a salacious smirk.

"No, but with you here, it feels wrong for some reason. I mean, if you want to explore a relationship with me, I shouldn't be having sex with your brothers."

"It's okay, we like to share each other's toys." His teasing snicker has me laughing but doubting his statement.

I look at him and ask, "Do you want to have sex with me today? I mean, if I'm being bad and experiencing new things, you're new."

He leans his face very close to me, his lips nearly touching mine. "Would you like to be with me?"

I can feel my body quivering. I whisper with a shaky voice, "I've always wanted to be with you."

A shock of wonderment rips across his expression a second before his warm, puffy lips press to mine. I've hoped for this since I was a little girl and the teacher introduced him as a new student to my class. I was only eight years old, but I had the biggest crush on him. Now, in this moment, I am his to do with as he pleases.

The heat from his palm on my cheek seems to radiate down to my breasts and further. My thighs instinctually squeeze together when my pussy twitches, alerting me that she wants him.

Our lips part, enabling him to pull off his shirt. As it falls to the floor, I'm shocked to see the large tattoo he has. It engulfs his left pectoral muscle up to his collar, over his shoulder and down his arm ending near his wrist. The detail is incredible, telling a story that I hope to learn in the future.

Fuck! He is thin but his chest is strong, abs are washboard ready and his arms bulge with muscles. It's obvious that he grew up slinging lumber in the woods with Patch and helping Mack build custom log homes.

"Wait, I want you in my mouth. I've dreamed of this moment for a long time, and I want to pleasure you first."

His face perks up in a sexy grin before he rises to his feet. With his eyes focused on mine, his jeans drop to his ankles followed by his underwear. A very large, stiff cock springs forth, ready for me to suck. He snickers when I gasp, shocked at its size.

"I get that reaction a lot."

I pry my eyes from his enormous prick long enough to glance up at his face. Since I was old enough to know what oral sex was, I've dreamed of what Bash would look like from this angle. The view is so much more thrilling than I had imagined it to be. He's even more desirable than I had thought possible.

"I heard the stories, but I didn't believe them. I mean, people sling a lot of shit when they've had a few drinks, most of which isn't to be taken at face value. I don't know if I can get much of it in my mouth."

"Changing your mind?"

I shake my head while studying his thick cock with my eyes, daring to clutch his prick in the tender grip of my palm. My hand looks small in comparison.

"You are so fucking beautiful. Do you have any idea of how many times I've jerked off at the thought of this exact situation? I don't think I can count that high."

"Really?" I ask, more shocked from the confession of his jerking off than the amount of times he claims he had.

"You really have no idea, do you?" Bash whispers with a crack in his voice.

His strong hand gently caresses my cheek while I look up at him. His expression has softened, erasing the roughness of his exterior to expose the emotion within him. He never struck me as a soft-hearted man, but I've only seen what he's allowed people to see. Right now, alone together, he's letting me see a side of him that not many likely do.

"Tell me," I whisper.

"You are the woman every man in this town has dreamed of making love to. When you walk into a crowded room, people take notice. Women are jealous of you and men dream of having you look at them the way you are looking at me right now. How am I so lucky to be here with you?"

My face slowly drops as I shake my head. "I'm not me today, not really. Casual sex is not something

I've ever done, and yet I was with both of your brothers. That makes me no better than a common slut, taking what I want and not caring who hurts from my actions. Doesn't it bother you that I was with them?"

"No, it doesn't. I share everything with my brothers and vice versa. We're close, very close. Since our parents died, it's only been the three of us. We rely on one another for everything in life. Patch's first girlfriend was the one who taught Mack and me how to please a woman. I'm grateful to her for those lessons. It's not uncommon for us to share women. Maybe one day that'll come to an end, but I hope not. I think it keeps us close."

For a moment, I imagine myself living here, dating Bash, and having sex with his two brothers any time the mood hits. My pussy twinges at the thought. It's the variety that has my womanhood damp. Each brother's cock is a different size, as are their bodies; each magnificent, strong and drool-worthy in its own way.

"Do you want me?" I ask with my eyes fixed on his.

We stare into one another's eyes for what seems like an eternity. He slowly leans down, lifting my chin with his finger. Ever so tenderly, his warm lips touch mine. My body instantly reacts. My nipples stiffen, and my thighs press tightly together. I want him, all of him, including his heart.

"Let me taste you," I whisper.

Bash stands tall, offering his thick prick for my pleasure. My hand is small against the thickness of his shaft. I kiss the tip, tasting a drop of his sticky arousal and I lick my lips before wrapping them around the head, teasing his pee-hole with my tongue and tasting his sex. A soft moan escapes him as I lean forward, taking as much of him as my stretched lips will allow. Fuck, his cock is huge!

I grip the base of his thick shaft firmly and suckle on as much of his length as I can manage to fit in my mouth. The spongy head of his shaft presses against the back of my throat and I want more, but my gaping mouth will only compensate so much.

I moan with delight when his heavy hand caresses my head. His thick fingers comb through my hair, pulling it off my face into a loose ponytail which he holds in his grasp. I'm grateful because now I can lick and suck him without my hair wrapping around his cock, thus making me gag. It's hard enough taking his size, I don't need any further intrusion making this more of a challenge.

Bash moans loudly and then pulls my mouth away from his engorged prick. He leans down, wrapping his strong arm around my back. He lifts me, pulling me with him as he crawls onto the bed above me. His mouth hovers over mine but he doesn't kiss me. Instead, his eyes meet mine.

"Goldie, I'm going to make love to you. I want your heart to belong to me. Your body is yours to share as you will, but never your heart, that's mine. Promise me."

A sensational warmth washes over me, leaving me feeling safer and more protected than I have ever felt. His eyes are kind, alluring and familiar in a way that doesn't seem possible. It's as if we've already shared a life together. Perhaps his yearbook photo is why but I feel like I've known him as my other half for years upon years. Is it possible to feel this close to someone I've seldom spoken with before today?

Our lips entwine as he lowers himself between my legs. His erection presses against my inner thigh. I've wanted him inside of me for so damn long. I shift my hips, but he moves with me, not yet allowing himself the pleasure of entering me just yet. His forearms rest above my shoulders, his fingers weaved into my hair. I could kiss this man all day, for the rest of my life and be very grateful to do so.

He lifts his face and his hips. The tip presses against the slick opening of my sex. I tilt my hips just enough to push the tip between my labia. Our lips part, readying for the moan soon to escape us both. He doesn't push in right away, he savors the moment while his eyes peer deeply into my soul.

Slowly, so slowly, he lowers his hips, burying himself completely. My eyes flutter, unable to remain linked to his. A long moan seeps from my core. At this very second, both my heart and body are being taken by this man.

"I'm yours," I whisper. "Please, don't hurt my heart."

"I've been waiting for you for so many years. I love you, always have. Hurting you … I never could."

His hips wave against me, pressing him so deeply into me that I think he may get stuck inside forever. I hope he does. I don't ever want him to slip out.

The room around us fades away as the friction between us seems to be building a fire deep inside of my belly. My hips leap up to meet his downward thrusts. With my legs wrapped around his thighs, I hang on, not letting him get too far away from me.

We are spinning out of control and my heart has given itself to him for safe keeping. Perhaps it was his all along and that's why I've never fallen in love. The lights have faded from my vision, only his face seems illuminated. My walls tighten around his thrusting shaft, begging him to never stop.

My fingernails dig into his back, begging him to take me! Take all of me! I'm fallen away now, lost in the vastness of my climax. My lids squeeze shut but my mouth gapes, willing to take in air if only my lungs should ever resume function. I'm frozen in time, stuck at the peak of my orgasm as his prick swells inside of me, stretching my already full vagina.

With a hard jerk, Bash spills his hot seed deep inside me. I cry out as I'm drawn back from my euphoria. My entire body shutters beneath him as the walls of my pussy twitch around his throbbing cock.

His eyes remain closed as the pained expression of orgasm eases from his face, replaced by a level of calmness I understand so well. Slowly, his eyes open to discover that I've been watching him.

We remain joined together as his sweet kisses ease away the tensions of my life. I could do this always, with him. With great regret, he rolls off me and onto his back, pulling me against him.

CHAPTER FOUR

I rest my head on Bash's tattooed shoulder. My finger traces the outline of the wolf's head that stares out from the left side of his chest, its teeth sharp as if protecting what hides beneath.

"Is the wolf here to protect your heart from women who want to break it?"

"It's there because it's already broken and vulnerable, so it needs to be protected."

I look up at his face, but he doesn't look at me. I ask, "Why is your heart broken?"

"When my parents died, it nearly destroyed me. It took a long time before I could even talk about them without a burning pain in my chest. The wolf is there to remind me that Patch will always protect me. The wolf on the back represents Mack, because he always has my back. If it weren't for Patch willing to watch over me, I would have ended up in foster care. He was only eighteen when they died."

"You were twelve. I remember the principle and guidance counselor coming into the classroom to get you. Nobody knew what was happening. When she whispered in Mr. Heavest's ear, his face fell sullen and his eyes darted straight at you. He wore an expression of pity. I just knew something bad had happened and it involved you. I wanted to go with you right then but was afraid to anger my parents. The teacher told us what happened after he was sure you were out of earshot. I cried all afternoon." The memory causes a lump in my throat and bringing tears to my eyes.

"Why did you cry? You didn't know my parents very well."

"I cried because I could imagine how much pain you were in. My parents were called to come pick me up and bring me home. I didn't know why it hurt me so much."

He places a kiss on the top of my head. I felt his pain that day, and still. I'll never forget it, as I'm sure that day will forever haunt him.

"I know they died in a car accident two weeks before the end of the school year, but what actually happened? You don't have to tell me if it's too painful. I've heard so many farfetched stories."

"Farfetched? Like what?"

"Well, one person said a Bigfoot ran out of the bush and they swerved to avoid it. Another said the truck driver, or the driver of the other car, was drunk.

Then some said your father was a mean son of a bitch and did a murder/suicide. I didn't believe any of them."

"Wow! A Bigfoot, huh? That's one I hadn't heard," he laughs.

"My parents wouldn't even talk about the accident. They said it would bring bad luck to speak of the dead. That made no sense to me. They simply told me to stay away from you boys because you were wild to begin with, and without parental guidance, the three of you were going to end up in prison or dead."

"Sounds like your parents never liked my family even when my folks were alive."

"Well, you didn't go to church three days a week and you boys hated wearing proper clothing like shirts and shoes." I roll my eyes and shake my head while my fingertips trace the valleys between his washboard abs. "So, what really happened?"

"They were on their way to get groceries when someone appeared to be trying to pass them on the highway. A witness said that woman was swerving all over the road just before she ran into the back of their car, sending them head-on into the grill of a semi coming in the opposite direction. They all died instantly. It was determined the woman who caused the accident was having a seizure and that's why she was driving so erratically. I take comfort knowing it was sudden death and they didn't suffer. The caskets were closed, so I didn't get to say goodbye. It's like I haven't had closure yet. Anyway, wolf tattoos are my brothers and they protect me."

"I'm sorry about your parents. That must have been very hard for you."

"It was harder on Patch than either Mack or me. Patch took on all the responsibility of raising us. Mack was sixteen, so he pretty much took care of himself, but I needed parenting. I regret giving Patch such a hard time. Maybe that's why we still argue a lot. If you keep touching me like that, I'm going to take you, hard this time."

"Is that so?" I ask, teasingly scratching my nails along the sensitive skin below his belly button.

"Do you think you can handle another fucking or is your pussy sore now?"

"I've had three men inside of me today, so yes, I'm a bit sore. It's wonderful but taxing. I should be getting home."

"I can walk you," he says as he sits up.

"No, you can't. If my parents see me with you … well, it won't be a good thing."

"True. Your dad might shoot me," he says with a jest.

Little does he realize my father just might. I'm his little girl and Bash is a Bear brother, a dangerous Satan worshipper who has soiled my good reputation. Well, they're probably right about that last part.

I slip my dress over my head and straighten it by gliding my hands down along my hips. Bash has his jeans on in no time. He arranges my boots so I can slip into them easily. I follow him through the living room. The unmistakably delicious scent of someone working hard in the kitchen fills my nostrils, making my mouth fill with saliva.

"Hey, what's for supper?" Bash asks Mack, who is standing over a pot holding a heavy ladle.

"Rabbit stew. Can you set the table? Goldilocks, you're staying for dinner," he insists without giving me the courtesy of posting it as a question.

"No, I can't. I wish I could, but I must get back. Thank you for the invitation. It smells great."

"Are you sure? You can call home to let your parents know you're here," he says as he offers up his phone.

I pull mine from the pocket of my dress, showing it to him. "I'm set, thank you. But no."

"She can't stay. Her parents would freak out if they knew she was here. They don't care for us all that much. We're wild boys, don't you know?"

"Wild boys?" Mack repeats as he drops the ladle in the pot and grabs Bash around his waist, pinning him against the wall as if wrestling in a professional cage match. "We are a bit wild."

Mack fakes a few punches to Bash's kidneys while they laugh.

"It's true, they think we're Satan worshippers because we don't go to church."

Mack releases him, tussling his hair in the process. "Well, we are doing our best to get their daughter into some trouble."

"Yeah, we're corrupting her with our bad-boy, seductive ways," Bash teases me with a wave of his eyebrows. I smile agreeing with him.

Patch walks up behind me, slapping me on the ass as he passes by. "You're both wrong. This hot, young thing is corrupting us."

Mack walks up to me and says, "Hell yeah she is! And, I for one, like it a lot." He kisses me gently on my lips and then looks me up and down. "I hope we get to play again soon."

My eyes shoot to see Bash's reaction but he's sampling the stew and adding salt while Mack is distracted. Patch grabs the spoon from Bash and pushes him out of the way so he can scoop up a taste for himself.

"I ... I don't know. Bash asked me to date him ... so, I'm not sure it's appropriate," I reply shyly.

Mack looks at Patch and then they both look at Bash. Mack asks, "Did you pee on her to mark her as your own?"

"I think he came on her, not peed on her, dumbass," Patch corrects him with his deep voice that vibrates my chest.

"He didn't do either," I reply. "He came inside me, not on me, and there was certainly no urine involved."

"It's not unheard of," Bash tells me with a look of expectation.

"What?" The look of shock on my face has all three of them laughing. "Oh, fuck off, all of you! Nobody does that!" I reply with a flushed face, embarrassed about my gullibility.

Patch kisses my forehead before whispering in my ear. "Some people are into golden showers, but you can relax, we aren't. I would really like to fuck you again before you leave for school. Come by any time."

My breath catches and I find myself biting my bottom lip. My face is flushing again, and my pussy is instantly hot and wet. He's a fun, hard fuck, and I want him again too.

"I'd like that, but it's up to Bash whether he wishes to share me or not," I whisper, but Bash and Mack both hear.

Bash takes my hand. "Goldie, you can fuck whoever you want. I told you that. I want your heart. The rest of you is yours to do with as you choose. If you want to fuck Patch and Mack right now, right here, it's your prerogative. I won't be upset. In fact, I might help out again."

All three of the smoking hot brothers are looking at me with their chests bare and bulges in their jeans. My mind is whirling with thoughts of having all of my three holes filled at the same time. I swallow hard. My face is still flushed but its cause isn't so much embarrassment as it is arousal. My pussy is dripping wet. I can feel my walls clench and it wakes me from my fantasy.

"I, um…" I clear my throat. "I have to go."

Bash reaches out for my hand and I join it. "I'll make sure she gets home safely. Keep supper hot for me."

"Take too long and we'll eat your share," Mack teases with a wink. "See you soon, Goldilocks."

"Bash can give you our phone numbers so you can call us any time the urge hits you." Patch's grin is wide and friendly, which seems unsuitable for his perpetually dangerous scowl.

"Thank you for … you know," I say, and then wave nervously as I slip through the doorway behind Bash.

As we walk, Bash says, "My brothers really like you."

"I like them too," I say with a crack in my voice.

"What are you doing tomorrow?" he asks as he takes a few wide strides and then starts walking backwards in front of me.

"Careful, you'll trip," I warn him.

"As long as you fall on top of me, I won't mind."

I smile and flutter my lashes in a nervous gesture. "I don't know what I'm doing tomorrow. Nothing is set in stone. My mother mentioned shopping for school supplies but I have everything I need, so I might just pass on that."

"You shouldn't," he says.

"Shouldn't what? Pass?"

"Yeah. She loves you and just wants to spend time with you before you move back to school."

"You're probably right. I'll go if she asks. I can say that I need a new laundry hamper or something."

He smiles and turns, slowing his pace until I am at his side. We walk hand in hand, in silence and lost in our own thoughts. I'm thinking about how hard and ruthlessly Patch fucked my pussy. And how Mack pleasured my clit with his mouth and then carefully slid his cock into my ass for my first time ever. But my thoughts are focused around Bash and the tenderness he showed me while our bodies and hearts became one. Even if our momentary love affair fades too quickly after I leave him, it will forever be instilled in my heart, totally and completely having taken me.

"Goldie, promise me that you'll come see me before you go back to school," he begs with sadness behind his words. His eyes look straight ahead as if looking at me will utterly destroy him if I should deny him his request.

"I promise to see you again before I leave. Maybe I'll visit your brothers again too, if you're sure that would be acceptable."

"Yes, Goldie, I'd like that too."

"Can I ask you why you call me Goldie and not Goldilocks?"

"Because nobody else does," he replies with a silly smile. "It'll be my pet name for you. Goldie. It has a nice ring to it. Don't you think?"

"Sure, why not? Normally I'd hate it but as long as you're the only Bear brother to call me Goldie, I'm okay with it."

"Do you not like the nickname?"

"I do as long as it's you're the one saying it," I reply after taking his outstretched hand so he can help me over a tree trunk that fell during the last storm.

"It's mine and only mine."

"When do you return to university?" I ask him.

"I only have one more course I'd like to take before I agree to graduate. I don't have to take it but I think it'll benefit me. It doesn't start for a few more weeks. How many credits do you need?"

"None, actually. I was wanting to go back to get a few extra credits. I'm worried I may not live up to the expectations of life. But now I'm rethinking that idea. I'd like to stay here with you. I won't because that would be ridiculous! I've worked my whole life for my education." I look at him and look away, wondering if I should confess something. "I didn't tell my parents this, and I hope it stays between us, but I already wrote the final exam to get my degree."

He looks at me with surprise. "You did? How did you do? And, the better question would be, why are you going back?"

"I wasn't ready to start my life, I suppose. I really like knowing that I can if I want to. Maybe I'm afraid to fail at real life. You probably think I'm an idiot."

"Of course not! You're a very intelligent woman, definitely not idiot material. So, if you're not taking classes, why return?"

"I'm signed up for additional classes to bump my qualifications."

"Do you not think you'll be a good nurse?"

"Of course, I do. I was working at the nursing home two blocks from my school and they've asked me to come on full time, but I don't know where I want to be. I have to decide whether to take that job offer, which is a good one, or look for something closer to my parents. I don't want to live with them forever and I fear that's what they'll expect if I decide to move back this way."

"Move in with us! There, issue solved!" Bash isn't laughing.

"Is that a joke?" I ask. "I think my parents would disown me or, at the very least call me a heathen."

"So?"

"I love my parents, but I don't think they'd accept that decision. Besides, before today, you hadn't said more than a dozen sentences to me, and all of a sudden you want me to move in? I don't think so."

"Well, the offer stands. Mack can design a log cabin for you on our property and you can live there rent free as long as you want. I can live in the big house with my brothers. No pressure!"

"That's very kind. Excessive, but kind. Why don't we take it a little slower than that, shall we?" I stop walking and turn to look at him.

"Slower? It took us fifteen years to get here. How much slower can we go?"

"Well, this is where I leave you."

"I know," he says, looking very disappointed that we've arrived near to my parent's home. "Give me your phone."

I hand it to him and watch as he puts all of their phone numbers in it. He hands it back to me with a silly grin.

"I named us Fucker, Eater, and Lover. That way, if your parents happen to look through your phone, they won't know it's us."

I roll my eyes and scan for their names. He really did use those titles. "Right, because Fucker, Eater, and Lover won't give cause for concern."

He laughs, kissing me once before turning me toward my parent's house and cracking my ass with his palm. I gasp, having not been expecting it. I rub it as I make my way across the yard. I'm sure he's laughing as he watches me try to soothe my butt.

"What's the matter with your bum?" my mother asks.

I jolt, not realizing she was standing behind the sheet hanging from the clothesline and swaying in the breeze.

"I fell and landed on my... do you need help?" I ask, hoping to change the subject before she can see through my lie.

"Sure!"

As we hang the remaining sheets, I catch her glancing at me more often than one should.

"What is it?"

"Hmm?" she asks, trying to seem innocently oblivious that she was staring.

"You're staring at me."

"Oh, it's nothing."

"Spill it, Mom!"

She turns to look toward the house as if making sure nobody is within earshot. "I know where you were and I'm all right with it, but don't tell your father."

"What?" I ask nervously. My body quivers with a strange childhood fear of getting caught. She can't possibly know where I was.

"You were with Bash Bear."

"H-how do you … what makes you think I was…" I look toward the trail that I just came from to see if he followed me into the clearing.

"I saw you with him. The trees aren't as thick and bushy as you might have thought. Besides, I heard him laughing as you came into the clearing. Don't worry; like I said, I'm not upset. You're an adult and can do as you please. Your father would disagree, however, so let's keep this between us."

"Um, okay. I'm … ah," I'm stumbling to find the right thing to say.

I had no idea my mother was so liberated in her new way of thinking. She's always hissed the Bear name when she spoke of them. Perhaps it's my father who doesn't like them and not my mother at all. I must be looking at her with a confused expression because she smiles.

"I had a flat tire up the road about three years ago. The rain was pouring in sheets and it was hard to see ten feet in front of me. I pulled over and got out of the car. I had the car up on the jack, but the wind was blowing and I was afraid the jack wouldn't hold. Just as I was about to take the spare from the trunk, Patch came walking up. I hadn't noticed that he'd pulled up and stopped behind my car. Like I said, it was raining heavily. He lowered the jack and tossed it back into the trunk of my car. He walked me to his car and opened the door. I climbed in and sat. Water was dripping from my hair and I was shivering. He started to drive me home but the big oak tree that used to be at the bend had fallen and blocked the road, so he took me to his house. I wasn't afraid of him like I thought I should be. He gave me some dry clothes and offered mc a hot shower, but I only took the clothes. He made us some tea and we sat at his kitchen table and talked while the storm passed. He earned my respect that day. Since then, we've chatted in passing."

"Did you tell Daddy?"

Her eyes widen. "Oh no! You can't tell him either!"

"I won't, I promise."

"So, you see, it's all right by me if you want to spend time at their place. I don't know the other boys but if Patch raised them, I'm sure they're respectful men. Are they?"

"Yes, they are. I got to know each one of them today," I'm not lying, "and they all were very good to me." Again, I'm telling the truth.

"You like Bash, then?"

I can feel my face flushing. "Yes, I've always liked Bash."

"I know. Mom's always know.".

CHAPTER FIVE

After dinner, I help tidy up and then soak my sore pussy and ass in the clawfoot bathtub filled to the rim with hot water, Epsom salts, and lavender oil. I breathe in the calming scent, but I'm too wound up for it to take effect. Picturing all three of them naked might have something to do with its failure.

Afterward, I slip on a nightie and flop on my twin sized bed, checking my phone to see if one of them has called but then remember that they don't have my number so it would be a small miracle if they had. I close my eyes for a moment and picture Bash Bear waiting at the end of his long driveway where the school bus would stop to collect him. My heart always beat a little faster when we rounded that corner and I'd see him hop off the huge tree stump wearing rip-knee jeans and a simple t-shirt with his backpack slung over one shoulder. He used to wear Mack's hand-me-downs until he grew taller than him.

I open my eyes and search my list of contacts for "Lover" and press the green dial icon. It rings only once before he answers.

"Hello, sexy woman. It took you awhile to miss me. I was wondering if you were ever going to call."

"It's only been two hours!"

"Yes, but I missed you. Mack said he wanted to put you up on the table and eat your pussy and ass for dessert but you left too soon. He said his tongue is lonely now. Come back! I'll meet you in the woods and bring you to our house for the night. I'll make sure you get back before sunrise. You might be exhausted by then, but I'll carry you home if I have to."

"That's an intriguing thought, but I'm going to have to pass."

He pulls the phone away from his mouth. "Hey Mack, she said she doesn't want your worthless, dried-up, abrasive tongue." He laughs.

"Hey! His tongue is marvelous," I whisper, hoping my parents don't hear me.

"Should I tell Patch you don't want his lame cock inside of you?"

"Um, no!"

"So, you do want his cock?"

"I ... wait, you're putting words in my mouth!"

"Words, cocks ... you choose," he jokes.

"What?"

"You said I was putting words in your mouth so you can either have words or cocks in your mouth. You choose."

"Smartass! I can't win with you, can I?"

"Sure you can! You can win over and over again but you have to be here for us to make that happen."

"That's not going to be possible tonight." I hear his exasperated exhale. "Did you know that Patch helped my mom with a flat tire and they had a lengthy conversation? I wonder if it went any further than that."

"He can be very seductive and irresistible, so I've heard." He pulls the phone away from his mouth again. "Hey, Patch! So you banged Goldie's mom?"

I hear mumbling in the background and then Bash start laughing.

"What did he say?"

"He's just teasing. Nothing happened between your mom and Patch. Can you picture it though? Your mom sprawled on the kitchen table while Patch nails her? Shit, I think I just grossed myself out."

"Eww!" I shake my head to remove the thought from my mind. "Keep talking like that and I'll never be in the mood for sex again!"

"Oh shit! We don't want that. I'll shut up. So, how did you find this out?"

"She told me after she said she saw me with you in the woods." Silence follows. "It's okay, she's not upset. That's when she told me about her chance meeting with Patch."

"What did your father say about us?"

"He doesn't know about Patch and my mom, or you and me. He wouldn't even try to understand."

"Okay, enough about your parents, my cock has gone soft. I much prefer to have it stiff with you being the cause. Tell me how many times you orgasmed today."

"Why, so you can jack off to my voice?"

"Yes, exactly," he replies with a chuckle.

"No phone sex. I think I've had enough new experiences for one day, thank you. However, I was considering coming to visit you tomorrow around noon. Mom wants to go shopping but said it's okay if I'd rather be with you. My father will be at work all day so she won't have to make up a cover story to tell him. If I simply walk away from the house, she won't know for sure where I'm going if he should care to ask her where I've been all day. Mom doesn't like to lie to my dad."

"We'd love to have you."

"We, or you?"

He chuckles. "You know I want you always. The guys would love to borrow you, if playing with them is something you'd like to do again."

"This sharing me idea will take some time to get used to," I confess.

"The option is there but not expected, and nobody would throw a temper tantrum if you don't want to play with them. Well, that's not completely true. Mack will whine like a toddler, but give him some cookies and he'll get over it soon enough."

"If the mood hits..." I don't finish my words because my pussy tightens at the thought of having all three of them naked and available at the same time. But then I wonder if I could even handle three men simultaneously invading my body.

"What's on your mind? You fell quiet all of a sudden."

"Um, nothing. I was just thinking." Again I pause too long.

"Thinking what?"

"Never mind, I don't think I could handle it anyway. Okay, so I'll stop in tomorrow. I'm not sure when exactly."

"Text me when you're getting ready to leave and I'll meet you halfway."

"You don't have to do that. I know my way around the forest."

"I know you do, but I'm a gentleman."

"Good night, Bash. Tell the boys I said to sleep tight."

"Goldie says to sleep tight." He pauses then laughs.

"What did they say?"

"Mack is in his room with the door shut now, but Patch said he'll sleep nice and relaxed tonight after giving you a good fucking."

"I doubt Patch will be relaxed since he didn't get to ejaculate." I'm glad he's not here to see me blushing.

He tells him what I said and then relays his reply. "Patch said he jerked off when he watched Mack fuck that sweet ass of yours, and that he'll be dreaming about the many ways he'd like to use your body."

"He did? I didn't know that," I reply, taking a few seconds to imagine him fucking his fist. "So, were you watching Patch jerk off?"

"Um, no! I don't prefer to watch my brother jerk off. He was standing behind me while I put my fingers in your pussy."

"You don't think it's weird to have your hand that close to your brother's cock?"

"I promise I didn't touch him. We're close but not that close. We drew that line in the sand a long time ago."

"I never understood that reference, 'drawing a line in the sand,' because sand is always shifting."

"Okay then, we drew that line in cement."

"I'll see you tomorrow. Good night Bash."

"Good night, lovely Goldie."

I hang up and then go downstairs to sit with my parents in the living room and join them in the silence as we each read for a while. After an hour and I've read the same page three times, I decide to go to bed. I'll need my sleep because I might require a lot of energy for tomorrow.

CHAPTER SIX

The sun is beaming too brightly for my tired eyes so early in the morning. The weatherman is calling for a severe storm in the early afternoon. I've been lying awake in bed for about an hour but I keep closing my eyes so I can better imagine the Bear brother's sexy eyes. If I look too eager to start my day by primping myself now, Dad will question my enthusiasm. Besides, it's too early to head over to the Bear house. I don't want to come across as being overzealous.

The seductive scent of coffee drifts into my nostrils, revving up my brain and urging me out of bed. I flip onto my back and recall the dream I had last night where I was looking into Bash's eyes while he was inside my pussy. One of the brothers was fucking my ass at the same time, but I'm not sure which one. I didn't want to tear my eyes away from Bash's loving gaze long enough to find out.

I sit up, stretch and yawn. As I walk to the door and pull it open, my nightie unravels. This is when I take notice of how dripping wet my pussy is. I quickly make my way to the bathroom to pee and clean myself up before heading to the kitchen to suck back half a pot of coffee.

The instant after Dad's car disappears down the driveway, my mom asks, "So what time are you heading over to the Bear house?"

"Are you sure you don't want me to come with you today? We could make it a girl's day."

"No, love. I want you to go have fun with your new teddy bear."

"Ha ha! I like the play on words, Mom. But are you sure?"

"Of course I'm sure. I want you to have fun with Bash. Let your hair down for once, Goldilocks. You're always so held together. Don't think I didn't notice how lazy and relaxed you seemed when you came home after being with that young man. I don't want to know what he did that led you there, I just want to see you happy. You were happy yesterday with him. You were never like that with anyone you've dated. It looks good on you." She brushes a lock of hair off my shoulder and then smiles while her eyes admire my face. "Yes, definitely more beautiful now."

"Thank you. I take after you."

"Hmm, maybe, but I can't take all the credit. When can you be ready?"

"I'll need a shower before I go."

"If you can be ready in fifteen minutes, I'll drive you. Otherwise you'll have to walk."

"I won't be ready by then. You go ahead. I enjoy the hike anyway."

"All right, bring the whistle with you."

"It's extremely rare to run into an actual bear but I'll bring the whistle anyway."

Mom jokes, "The Bear brothers look scarier than any bear I've ever seen."

"Well, Patch looks scary. Mack and Bash look dangerous but in a seductive way."

"Is there something you aren't telling me?"

"What?" Does she somehow know that I've had all three of them inside my body? No, there's no way she could know that.

"Have a great day. I'll see you for dinner?" She poses that statement more like a question, but I know better than to be late.

"I'll be here, or I'll call in advance."

"If you don't, your father will question your whereabouts."

"I know. I'll keep tabs on the time."

After my shower, I skip the bra and panties, choosing to slip on a halter top and a free-flowing short skirt. As soon as my hair is pulled into a high ponytail,

I give my reflection a once over in the mirror and head off to the Bear residence.

I didn't text Bash to let him know I was on my way because I know how to get there and decide to surprise him instead. He needs to realize I'm a strong woman who doesn't need a male escort. This forest is where I grew up. I know it well and enjoy the solitude its foliage provides.

I'm lost in thought about the possible coming events when the sound of a cracking branch nearby startles me back to reality. My feet halt in place. All I can hear is the thunderous pounding of my heart. I scan left and right, trying to hear every sound that isn't typical of the lonely forest.

I hear it again and spin around to look behind me. My eyes are wide as they peer into the dark shadows cast by the roots of the fallen trees, each one taking on the shape of a rather large bear. I suddenly regret not bringing the whistle. I can picture my mother yelling at me while I lie dead in a casket. My fucking heart is so goddamn loud!

The noise has stopped. I should continue the trek to the Bear house making double time, keeping my senses more aware of my surroundings. I take a deep breath while scanning the area one more time. Nothing is moving that shouldn't be but my knees are shaking.

I spin and slam face first into something hard. A scream lodges in my throat but the hard landing on my backside jerks it loose. I hear running behind me but my legs are like cooked pasta noodles with no strength to lift my body. I can't run away from whatever is after me.

A large human hand grabs my forearm, yanking me to my feet. My mouth is suddenly covered by another hand, muffling my screams. I open my eyes to see Patch, blurry and standing in front of me with a wickedly sexy sneer.

"Do you want to play rough, Goldilocks?"

My heart is on fire from trying to break itself free from my chest. My glare should alert him that I'm not impressed with them having hunted me, but he doesn't seem to care in the least. I'm furious that he gave me such a start and I want him to know it. I can't turn to see who's holding me hostage because I'm not able to spin my head. It is held back against a strong chest by a hand over my mouth. My right arm has been pulled behind me and is being restrained unnecessarily high. When I groan in protest, it's lowered but not released.

"I asked you a question, Goldilocks, and I expect an answer," Patch says with a deep and seductive voice.

My anger is subsiding and I can think clearer now that my adrenaline isn't flooding my brain. I nod my head slowly. My curiosity about what they have planned for me has my pussy tightening. I'm desperate to know who's behind me, but sort of hoping the answer isn't revealed until after I'm fucked by the stranger. The uncertainty has my nipples pressing hard against my soft cotton halter top.

"He's going to release your mouth and you're not going to scream. Are you? It doesn't matter if you do, nobody will hear you this far into the woods." I try to say that I won't, but my voice halts behind the hand. "Have you ever had a rape fantasy?"

I shrug my shoulders. I have but saying it out loud seems wrong. Too many women and men are raped, so a fantasy of it happening to me shouldn't be arousing even if it's only a game. I don't want anyone to have sex with me without my consent, but the idea of someone I'm willing to play with taking me while I play the helpless victim sounds rather thrilling.

"We don't often call it rape because rape refers to non-consensual sex and we'd gladly destroy someone for doing that. Nobody would ever find their body. But, back to what I was saying. We call it consensual non-consent. That means that we pretend it's against your will, but you have a safeword in case it gets too hairy for you. Are you willing to play along?"

I nod my head.

"Red will be the word that makes everything stop immediately. If you say it, we will let you go, and no one will touch you in a sexual manner after that. Do you understand?" I nod. "Let's get started, shall we?"

***

My arms are pulled around in front of me by the man at my back. They're held together while Patch begins skillfully wrapping a thick rope around them in a rather appealing design. He ties it off. The hands release my arms, giving me the opportunity to turn but Patch tugs the rope, redirecting my attention. I step forward with a nervous giggle. I've never been bound before. It's scary and that makes it seem so taboo. I seem to like taboo lately.

The rope is looped around an overhanging tree branch and pulled taught. My body is stretched tall. My boots rest comfortably on the mossy foliage, but my arms are raised high over my head. I can't go anywhere. Again, nervous laughter.

Patch smirks and then grasps my top, pulling it up to expose my breasts. He lifts it until it covers my eyes. I can't see but the rope keeps me from losing my balance and toppling over. My skirt is yanked down, and each boot is lifted until the material and boots are freed from my body. My bare feet rest on the cushioned layer of soft moss. I remain nude, blind, and vulnerable for all to see.

My heart is throbbing and I can just barely see the moving human shapes through the tight fabric weave. A figure I recognize to be Bash is a few feet away from me and taking off his pants. I turn my body so I can get an idea of who's around me and that's when I see two more figures. One is Mack and the other Patch. Mack is sitting on a rock or stump behind me, but not undressing. Patch stands behind me, folding my skirt.

"I'm going to be rough with you." Patch's deep voice vibrates my chest like the roar of a powerful motor.

"Rough? Like how?" I ask, suddenly rethinking this bondage/consensual non-consensual game I've agreed to play.

Patch's unmistakable voice comes from directly behind my head. "Spanking, pinching, swatting."

"Swatting?" I ask in barely a whisper.

"With a switch taken from a tree. It stings and will likely leave red welts on your body, but they'll go away."

"I don't think I'll enjoy the switch." My heart is pounding furiously again.

"I'll let you know when it's coming and you can decide if you don't want to try it, or be a brave little girl and give it a try. If you don't care for it, you can say orange and I won't use it again."

He presses his hot chest against my back and glides his fingers down my tummy, sending shivers that stiffen my nipples. They slowly ease their way down between the slippery folds of my pussy, and begin gently stroking my clitoris.

"I'll reward you well if you take the punishments."

"What if I scream?"

"Your screams are my reward. No one will hear your desperate pleas, so scream until your mouth runs dry. Just remember your safewords. What are they?"

"Orange and red," I tell him with a mouth that suddenly feels very dry.

"Saying yellow means you've reach your intensity level. Do you understand?"

"Yes, I do."

"I'll start with a spanking using my hands. I'm going to swat you twelve times. Eight of those will be on your ass."

"And the other four?"

"You'll see," he replies in his typical stern and assertive manner.

I feel safe with these men, even though one of them is about to physically hurt me, something I never thought I'd permit a man to do. His fingers leave my pussy, disappointing me.

"Open your mouth and taste your excitement."

I do as instructed, opening wide. His fingers slip into my mouth and I close my lips around them, sucking my flavor from each digit. He pushes them deeper into my mouth, so far I fear I may gag. Ever so slowly he retracts out.

"I want you to count the spanks. All of them. If you miss one, I'll add two to the count."

His hand cracks down on my right ass cheek and I yelp. My heart is pounding so hard in my chest that it might break free!

"You aren't counting. This is your one warning."

The figure I'm fairly sure to be Bash stands a few feet in front of me and I believe he's stroking his cock. He's watching Patch punish me and it's arousing him.

"One," I retort. Another crack on the same cheek. I immediately yell, fearing he'll add another. "Two!"

The anticipation of the third has me quivering. He pauses, remaining still and silent. I jolt when his fingertips brush across the burning handprints on my ass. I wait for another touch, not knowing if he'll spank me or touch me tenderly. The anticipation of it builds butterflies in my tummy.

Crack! Yelp! "Three!" Another immediately follows. "Four." The final two alternate ass cheeks. "Five, six!"

I'm gasping, tears welling up behind the makeshift blindfold.

"Your ass is turning a lovely shade of pink and I can see my giant handprints on your shapely ass. It's making my dick hard." He pushes his bare, rock-hard cock between my tightly squeezed legs. I tilt my hips toward him. I want him inside of me.

"Eager little bitch, aren't you? You're so fucking wet!" he purrs behind my left ear.

He reaches around me, cupping both of my breasts in his slap-happy palms. His hot fingers pinch my nipples, gradually increasing the intensity of the pressure, making me cry out. I'm wiggling to get away but it's useless. He has them held firmly. The more I squirm, the harder he pinches and tighter he holds me against his chest.

I whimper, hoping he'll take pity on me. He doesn't. Instead, while he squeezes my nipples, he pulls them as if he's trying to rip them from my breasts. I scream when the pain is too great. He releases them and then tenderly rolls them between those same punishing fingers. This feels really good, surprisingly hypersensitive to his touch immediately after the inflicted pain.

Bash walks toward me and the silhouette of his thick, erect prick swings with each step. He has a great cock. Having him inside of me makes me feel full, but it's more than just a physical fullness. It's a total mind-altering feeling that I can't explain. All I know is I want more of that, more of him.

He slides the halter top higher up on my arms to expose my mouth, leaving my eyes shielded, and then presses his to mine. He has the softest lips of all the brothers and his kisses are more tender despite his efforts to seem aggressive. Even in the height of his passion, when most men's kisses are more eager, his puffy lips are like pillowed bumpers, protecting me from the harshness of the assault.

Bash slips his fingers between my sex, quickly finding my clitoris. His easy circles rim the hood in a tantalizing tease. I moan softly into his mouth.

Whack! Whack! I scream. The sharp burning of my ass cheeks combined with the arousal of my clitoris is thrilling!

"Count," Bash whispers.

It takes me a moment to remember what number I'm at. "Ah … seven, eight," I manage.

My hips tilt toward Bash's hand, pleading with him not to stop. His fingers slip further back and into my pussy. With the palm of his hand pressing against my clit, I'm coming closer and closer to orgasm. I hump against it, taking his fingers into me while simultaneously arousing my clit. I'm so fucking close!

He pulls his hand away just before my climax erupts. I beg and plead but he only steps away from me. Patch takes Bash's place in front of me. He's just as tall as Bash but so much larger and therefore more intimidating. I like the fear his size awards me, especially when I can't get away. I know I'm safe, so the fear is more of a thrill than anything.

"Spread your legs wide," he tells me, while caressing my silky breasts with his gruff hands.

I do as he's instructed but only able to spread my legs about shoulder width, otherwise I'll be on my tiptoes. I'm sure to step cautiously on the soft moss. Getting a stick poked in the bottom of my foot would be a mood wrecker for sure. I stand with my legs apart. The cool air caresses my hot, swollen clit.

"I'm going to spank your pussy."

"No!" I shout. Before I can close my legs in protest, his thick hand swats my pussy lips, stinging my clit like a bolt of electricity zapped me.

I shriek from the shock of the sting and don't want another, not yet anyway. My legs are shaking so hard I can't lift them to pull them closed. Instead, my knees buckle inward, shifting my weight and putting more strain on my wrists.

"Open your legs or I'll add another. Don't forget to count." His words ring loudly in the quiet forest, even though they were spoken in his normal tone.

"Nine," I whisper. Realizing it wasn't as painful as my mind had lead me to believe, I do as he orders, spreading my legs as wide as before.

"Ready?" I bite my bottom lip, as if that will make what's to come less shocking.

Slap! My pussy stings and burns. He doesn't remove his hand after that slap, which seems to make the pain dissipate quickly because of his hand's heat. Two of his fingers easily slide into my drenched hole, burrowing so deeply into me that I can feel his knuckles pressing against my opening. I'm not surprised by how soaking wet I am.

He waves inside of me, wickedly assaulting my g-spot. The speed of his movements have me coming in a matter of seconds. I wail through a powerful orgasm that begins deep inside my body and finishes with a blast of my hot cum coating his hand. It continues to spirit, splashing against my thighs, tickling my flesh as it trickles downward. His fingers withdraw, leaving me panting and shaking.

He slaps my right tit, likely thinking I won't enjoy it, but I do. *Swat!* "Ten!" I scream with a taunting laugh quickly following. I push my chest toward him, inviting another. I'm so fucking turned on that he could slap me anywhere and I'll likely invite him to do it again.

Another slap, this one to my left tit. *Slap!* "Eleven!" I growl in a very uncivilized way. I've always thought of myself as a lady with very feminine tendencies but right now, I'm a horny bitch with a need for satisfaction.

Swat! I lurch toward him and scream, "Twelve! Fuck me!"

Bash rushes behind me, grasping my hips in his tough hands and lifting them until I'm balancing myself on my tip-toes. He lines up his cock and rams its full length into me, forcing the breath from my lungs with a loud, appreciative moan.

He pounds himself into me with a fierceness that I'd been hoping for. My head is spinning, the darkness is pulling me further from reality as orgasms ripple through me, one after another. I have no concept of how long he fucks me, but it seems like forever yet not long enough. He slides his gorgeous prick from my twitching cunt and I whine like a child who dropped their sucker in the dirt. "More!"

My hands are untied and set free. They feel heavy and tingle as my blood rushes through them. The shirt covering my eyes is yanked off, but I can't seem to open my lids. The brightness of the sun has me squinting as my lashes shield my protesting eyes.

My hair is grabbed and I'm forced onto my knees. After my head is yanked back, a cock is shoved between my parted lips. Whomever it is is fucking my mouth quickly but not deeply. I wrap my lips around it and suck as it pulls and pushes. The sound of someone to my right unzipping his pants seems very loud.

The hand releases my hair, but another quickly takes its place. I can tell it's someone else because of the easiness of this guy's hair-pulling. This man isn't as brutish in his guidance. His cock pushes into my mouth and I can tell it belongs to Mack. Its smaller size gives him away. It's long but thinner than his brothers' pricks. He glides in and out of my mouth as my lips encircle him.

My hair falls free, but I continue to ravish Mack's hard cock. My forehead bounces against his strong belly as I take him deep into my throat, amazing myself with my ability to control my gag reflex. His moan is lengthy and appreciative of my talent.

Two hands grasp me under my arm and I'm suddenly being lifted to my feet. This is disappointing; I wanted to make Mack cum down my throat. Mack lines up my boots for me to step into, wiping the dirt and moss from my soles before guiding them in.

Bash takes my hand and walks me over to where Patch is standing, fiddling with a rope. I can finally see clearly without the sun burning my eyes. Seeing three extremely handsome, well-built men walking naked through the forest with their stiff cocks wagging free in the breeze has my pussy twitching. I want them, all of them.

CHAPTER SEVEN

Patch waves me toward him. He stands on the opposite side of a downed tree. The trunk is thick and level at my hips. I stand with my hands resting on its bark, admiring its texture.

"Give me your hands," he instructs.

Without hesitation, I lift them and put them together just as they were before. He binds them with a slight difference from the last time. He slowly pulls the rope, forcing me to step forward until I'm leaning over the trunk. My tummy rests on the scratchy bark. It's not very comfortable, that's for sure.

He squats down, tossing the rope ends through a gap under the trunk. I feel it hit my boots. My calves are wrapped separately using each end of the rope. I can move my feet wider apart but can't step back without my hands being pulled further beneath the trunk. I'm bound around this tree, vulnerable and unable to fight back—not that I'd want to.

Large hands separate my ass cheeks and then a thick cock is pushed between my slick pussy lips until its forced deep inside me. Bash pounds into me and all I can do is lie here and take it. The warm bark digs into my soft skin, scratching its top layer. It hurts but it's adding to the whole experience. Oh fuck! This is so incredible!

Just before I cum, he pulls out of me, leaving me panting and grunting in protest. Another cock is buried into me and this time I know its Mack's. He slides easily in me. His cock being slimmer allows for me to focus on its firm tip poking at my cervix with each thrust. I like it, a lot. He also isn't kind enough to let me cum.

He pulls out and is quickly replaced by Patch. His thrusts are relentless and much more powerful than those of his brothers. The thunderous pounding of his thick thighs is painful, but I want more. The bark feels like it's cutting into my skin, but I don't care. At this point, I'd let a wild horse fuck me. Without giving him any warning, I start coming—hard.

He yanks his cock out of me and cracks my ass with a widespread hand, reigniting my burning ass cheek. The sting is incredible, more electric than before. It adds another level of intensity to my already, all-consuming orgasm, ending it with my shrieking wail that echoes back at me from the deepest pockets of the surrounding forest.

As I gasp to catch my breath, something long and thin trails down my spine. My head jerks up, turning as if I'll be able to catch a glimpse of what it is.

"It's a switch," Patch informs me.

"Are you going to hit me with that?" I pant.

"Yes, I'm going to swat you five times. If you accept all of the swats without telling me to stop, we will all fuck you until you can't discern one cock from the other. Are you ready?" Patch explains.

"This is going to hurt a lot, isn't it?" I ask, not really needing him to confirm what I already know.

"Yes, but you might like it," Bash suggests. He's standing several feet behind me.

Patch swats me with the switch and it fucking hurts. The sharp sting overwhelms me. I can't scream. I was expecting the pain but when it tears through my body the way it does, my mind snaps back to reality. I'm no longer lost in the delirium of an orgasmic fog.

"Breathe, Goldilocks," Patch instructs. He places a warm hand on the small of my back and it helps to ground my mind. I inhale slowly, letting it out in silence. He rubs my lower back. "Prepare for another, a little harder."

Twack! Aargh! My head is spinning. I've never felt anything so abrupt in my entire life.

"Take in the pain. Absorb it. Don't let it overwhelm you." Patch is leaning over me, whispering in my ear. "You are stronger than your pain."

I breathe slowly, my eyes blinking away the eruption of tears that are starting to blur my vision. To stop them from building, I close my lids. I nod slowly, letting him know I'm ready for more. Two down, three to go.

The third swat hurts like hell but I don't cry out. I'm trying to take his advice, to absorb the pain and not allow it to overwhelm me. I'm shaking, thankful the ropes are holding me in place, otherwise I'd be on my ass.

Another *whack!* I wasn't ready for this one. I scream, letting the pain escape me through my voice. The sound of my scream drifting into the thickness of the forest draws my mind away with it.

Another crack, this time harder than all the others. My wail is that of a woman lost in her pain. The sound seems to come from someone else, not me, definitely not me. This woman's voice sounds different; deeper and more animalistic.

My ass is caressed, each welted scar from the switch traced with the feathery touch of a tongue. Fuck! It hurts but my pussy is tightening, begging to be touched, licked or fucked. I can't focus my thoughts on any one particular thing. It's as if I've left myself; my inhibitions, fears and insecurities and escaped to a freer state of existence.

Suddenly, my pussy is plundered with a very hard cock. Mack stabs at my cervix, thumping against it in a sensational way that forces me quickly into orgasm. Oh yes! I want more!

His hips bounce off my sore ass cheeks, but I don't care how much they hurt or how the bark scraping the flesh on my body irritates. I want to be filled, to feel the closeness of a warm body. I want Bash!

Mack humps erratically, groaning and panting like a man taking his pleasure. His prick pulls from me, but I hear the whimpering sounds men tend to make when they orgasm, and it pleases me to know that my body was a vessel he used to give himself that much pleasure.

Patch slams his thick dick into me and immediately begins humping into me like a wild animal taking what's his. My pussy spasms around his cock within seconds. I'm overwhelmed, lost in another orgasm, and then another and yet another. I hear him cry out just before his thickening prick yanks from my depths.

At some point, and I don't know when, my ankles and wrists were untied. I could have moved at my own will, had I chosen to. If I had, I'd have been a fool to deny myself this pleasure.

I'm lifted off the fallen tree and carried in a pair of strong arms. My body is laid down on the mossy patch beneath the tree branch I was hanging from originally. It seems like it began so long ago.

Bash's lips press to mine, and the world seems to disappear around us. My arms wrap around his neck, holding his face to mine so my lips can easily reach his. The softness of his hot skin feels like cotton compared to the roughness of the warm tree bark.

He slips his huge cock into me and rests his hips between mine. Instead of fucking me, he holds himself inside me while he lovingly kisses me. His breath fills my lungs and mine his. He is mine, the one I truly wanted. The others don't matter, they're only bodies there for the purpose of my entertainment.

My legs fall open listlessly. His hips gently roll between my thighs, burrowing his hot thickness deep into my soul. My fingers weave into his thick, dark hair. We are panting together, loving the way our bodies move perfectly to complement each other's motion.

My thoughts are fading into darkness as I allow myself to drift away with him. It is only us that exist. We are here together as one. Nothing matters—life and death are irrelevant. I only want to feel the way his heart is thumping harshly in his chest in perfect sync with mine.

"Goldie," Bash whispers under his breath.

My tired legs wrap around his back, ankles linking together to pull him in deeper. Our bodies mold into one. I don't know where I begin and he ends.

There is no him and I, it is only us—one being—one heartbeat—one mind.

"I have always loved you," he whispers.

I'm spinning, barely able to keep myself from being thrown off the earth. Our bodies are welded together as if we fear being torn apart by some strange, unforeseen force. His hands clutch either side of my face. His lips continue to touch mine, but not in a traditional kiss. Our breath is one. If he pulls away, neither of us will be able to breathe and we will die. He needs me. I need him.

I've become very small and insignificant beneath him. I just know I am forever lost to this man. A warmth rushes over me, followed by the most amazing orgasm I have ever had the good fortune to experience. His pleasure is also mine. His seed spills into me as wave after wave of the most incredible emotional and physical euphoria overcomes us both.

We lay here, locked together on the mossy floor until his withered manhood slips from my depths, disconnecting our souls. We both sigh heavily as if the separation is excruciating.

His head lifts enough so he can look into my eyes. "I meant what I said, Goldie. I love you, always have. From the first time I saw you, I knew you'd be mine one day."

"I was always drawn to you, too. I just thought it was a childhood crush. It's so much more, isn't it?"

"Yes, for me anyway." His eyes search my face for any doubt that our feelings are mutual.

When a smile creeps up on my face, his expression softens. My hands slowly glide down his sides. He twitches as if ticklish. I giggle and purposefully tickle him.

"That's enough of that!" he says, lifting his tired body off me. I suddenly feel very cold and alone.

Bash helps me sit up and that's when I realize just how weary and well-used my body feels. I look around expecting to see Patch and Mack watching us, but they are nowhere to be found. I'm relieved that our bonded lovemaking wasn't witness by anyone, shared for future ridicule should one of them choose to poke fun at the most favored moment of my life thus far.

I stand on wobbly legs and giggle at how depleted I am of energy. As soon as my hands touch my ass, I'm reminded of the punishment I was given.

"Does it hurt a lot?"

"No, it's not so bad that it'll annoy me. Each time I sit down tonight I'll be thinking about it, and maybe tomorrow too. Does it look bad?"

He ganders at my ass but doesn't say anything, he just continues to stare.

"Well?" I ask impatiently.

"You might not think it looks okay but to me, it's sexy as hell."

"Do you like seeing red lines on my skin? Does it turn you on?"

"I like it because it reminds me how your face looked after each swat. You were so strong, and you overcame. Disciplining you isn't my thing, but Patch really gets off on it. Mack enjoys how aroused some women get from it and I've learned to appreciate it."

"Appreciate it?"

He shrugs, "Yeah. I've been told that the pain and arousal that comes from it can take a person deep into themselves, leaving them feeling emotionally, physically and mentally fulfilled."

"Have you ever been whipped?"

"Patch took a switch to me the day I took his truck out for a joyride and dumped it in the creek." He scratches his head and smiles as if recalling the memory of that day brings him joy. "I didn't enjoy it though. He really let me have it. I remember how those purple lines on my ass burned for days. I tried to make him feel guilty for it but he only smiled at me. He told me he'd gladly whoop me again if I ever needed a refresher."

"He must've been overwhelmed suddenly being the guardian of his two younger brothers. You guys weren't exactly well-behaved boys."

"Yeah, trouble always found us. One day when Patch got angry and stormed off into the woods, I followed him. When I caught up to him, I saw him crying like a desperate man needing help. He was begging for someone to help him, but nobody was around to hear him other than me. I just remember how he looked so small despite his massive size. That's when I realized how hard we were on Patch. That moment changed me."

"Did you ever tell him you were there?"

He shakes his head as he pulls up his jeans. "Hell no. That was a private, desperate time in his life. We all have at least one. I didn't tell Mack either. If I'd have brought it up to Patch, he would've stopped his façade of being the strong parental figure we needed him to be. He didn't have to know I saw his vulnerability. Why am I'm telling you all of this?"

"What about Mack? What was he like growing up?"

"How did he seem to you?"

I think back, trying to remember what my perception of Mack was, but I didn't really know him very well. Since he was a few years older than me, I didn't share classes with him either. I only saw him getting off the school bus and lighting a cigarette before walking up the driveway. I can't smell smoke on him now so I'm sure he quit.

"He always seemed to be sad. He didn't talk much but the girls were always hot for him. Then again, they were for you too, and Patch."

He snickers, sarcastically saying, "Fuck yeah! They all wanted a piece of the hot Bear brothers." I shake my head and roll my eyes at his feigned attempt at egotism. "Mack was a depressed teenager. I think he got into trouble just so someone would give him attention, even if it was the wrong type of attention. Patch took pity on Mack because he was Mom's favorite. She took him everywhere and he loved it. Dad usually had Patch by his side and I always tagged along with them. Mack had the hardest time adjusting after they died."

"And what about you?"

"What about me?"

"What are your future plans?"

"Well, I have to finish one course at school and then I suppose I'll write a book, maybe about our adventures. I'll never leave this forest though. This is my home and I'll live and die here."

Bash walks me most of the way home and then kisses me before sending me on my way. The rain is just starting to fall, creating the sound I refer to as the forest's orchestra. I love this sound but the darkness that comes with it is quite eerie.

CHAPTER EIGHT

My father is already home from work by the time I walk in the door. Unfortunately, my mother isn't. As far as he knew, I was supposed to be with her today.

"Where's your mother?"

"Um, I'm not sure. I walked home."

"From the city?"

"No, I was just walking." Why am I lying to my father? I'm a grown woman.

"To where?" His expression has changed from curiosity to irritation.

"I was at the Bear residence." There it is! I stand before him, waiting for his wrath.

After he clears his throat, I watch his Adam's apple bob when he swallows down his anger. "Well, you're a grown woman who can make her own decisions. I thought you were intelligent enough not to lower yourself to be with a Bear boy. They're so beneath you, Goldilocks. They'll only tarnish your good name and reputation."

"Don't you mean *your* good name and reputation? I'm no better than them. Had you two died in a car crash, I wouldn't be nearly as strong or self-sufficient as they are."

"Do not compare yourself to them. They have a long list of criminal behavior that will follow them their entire lives. You will stay away from them if you know what's good for you!"

"Is that a threat?"

"Take it as you will. Whichever scumbag you're about to give yourself to will only use your body and throw you away. Each one of them is a filthy, vulgar boy in a man's body. You will stay away!"

"I favor Bash, the youngest one. He's a wonderful man with a great future in front of him. He's about to graduate university, in case you didn't know. He has a strong future and he's good to me. Maybe he has a criminal record. I don't know, and I don't care. I feel safe with him, safer than I ever did with the other guys I've dated. Bash actually wants to make me happy. Nobody else ever cared or respected me enough to ask what I wanted. I'm not going to stop seeing him, Daddy."

"If you don't stop seeing him, I won't support you any longer. You'll have to finish school on your own and you won't be welcome in my home. He's bad for you, Goldilocks. I love you and only want what's best for you, and that boy is not it."

"You're kicking me out?" I'm shocked that he would cast his only child aside so easily.

"No, I'm asking you to choose between a promising future and a future loaded with disappointment."

Dad stands up, taking a deep breath and letting it out slowly. I can see the distress in his eyes and it's breaking my heart. Why doesn't he trust my opinion of Bash? I've heard most of the rumors involving the Bear brothers and some I believe to be true, but most are embellished tales to intrigue the gossiping townsfolk. But they would never hurt me. They would defend me if I needed them to. I'm sure of it.

"I feel sorry for you, Daddy. I'm sorry you don't trust me enough to make the choices that are best for me. If I'm to fall, let me fall. You raised me to be strong and independent. Now that I am, you don't like it. I love you but if you won't even try to see things from my perspective, I don't know what else there is to say."

I walk to my room and quickly pack what I'll need into a backpack while choking back tears. The only sounds I hear coming from the other side of my bedroom door is the kettle's obnoxious whistle.

My father is standing at the counter with his back to me when I enter the kitchen, hoping he'll tell me that he was wrong and will try to get to know Bash. But, he doesn't. He doesn't even turn around.

With a soft voice, I say, "I wonder what Mom is going to say about this. They're good, hardworking men, Dad. You should reconsider your intolerance. I'm sure you'd like them if you were to have a conversation with them."

I stand in the silence waiting for something, anything. He sighs heavily but keeps his back to me.

"Daddy, I'm twenty-three years old. Mom was twenty-one when you two married. She was twenty-two when I was born. Are you saying she wasn't wise enough to know you were a good man? Grandpa didn't like you much back then. Mom told me that he begged her not to marry you, but she knew differently. She knew you were good for her. Okay, I'm leaving now. Do you have anything to say?"

Silence.

"I love you, Daddy."

I push open the screen door and walk out, letting it slam behind me. I half expect him to chase after me, his one and only child, but he doesn't.

Evening is setting in and getting darker as I enter the forest. The shadows all look like creatures that are ready to eat my flesh whether I'm dead or not. It's eerily quiet except for the scuffling of my boots on the path. I feel safe here but when I look into the thicket of the trees, knowing I have to walk that way leaves me a bit uneasy.

I dig through my pockets and then the backpack for my phone. It's nowhere. Dammit! I left it on the dining room table along with my keys. Looks like I'll be going it alone.

The thought of an animal chasing me down and eating me has my knees shaking. As proven earlier, I'll likely be too afraid to attempt to outrun a hungry animal. Mom will believe I'm at Bash's. Bash will think I'm home, ignoring him for whatever reason. Maybe he'll find my remains. Hopefully the scene is not too gory.

I listen with a sharp ear while searching the shadows of the forest for anything large and carnivorous. My tiny flashlight just isn't strong enough to cast sufficient light to reflect the eyes of a hungry beast. During the fifteen-minute walk, I trip twice, cursing my clumsiness each time. When I come to the open path, I start to walk quicker, less fearful of uneven ground.

Their house is quiet with only the sound of a television breaking through the silence of the night. I shouldn't be here. What if Bash wants me to stay but his brothers don't? Worse yet, what if my father is right?

My knuckles tap lightly on the heavy wooden door as my broken heart races. The television quiets so

I rap again, louder this time. I clear my throat when Mack opens the door.

"Did you come back for more?" he teases, ending with a quirky grin.

"No, my father kicked me out."

His smile sags. "Well, come on in then." He stands aside, allowing me to walk through. "Here, let me take that." I hand him my backpack and he set it on the table.

Patch strolls out of his room, which is right off the kitchen. "What's going on?" He looks concerned.

"Her father kicked her out." Mack shrugs.

"You didn't tell him what we did to you this afternoon, did you?" Patch grins.

"Hell no! If I had, he'd be here with his gun cocked and ready to take you all to your graves."

"I hope your pussy isn't too sore from earlier," Patch says with a crooked grin.

I smile shyly. "No, it's fine."

"So, what happened with your father?" Patch asks while pulling out a kitchen chair and offering it to me. He picks up my backpack and puts it in his room while Mack grabs a few beers from the fridge, handing one to each of us. I look around but don't see Bash, but the bathroom door is closed.

"He asked where I had been all day so I told him I was with Bash. He said that I shouldn't be seen with you hoodlums because you're a bad influence and you'll ruin my innocence."

Patch is quick to remind me that's not so. "As I recall, you came here begging me to take your innocence."

"Yes, I remember. He knows I'm not innocent, but he doesn't like the reputation associated with the name Bear. Now that I'm an adult, I don't think he should tell me who I can't spend my time with."

Patch takes a long slug from his bottle. "And what did you mother say about it?"

"She wasn't home. She'll be so angry with him when she finds out. Of course, I doubt she'll tell him about you rescuing her on the side of the road that rainy day."

"You know about that?"

"I do. She told me," I reply.

This is obviously news to Mack. "What? You rescued her mom? When was this and how did I not hear about it?"

"It was nothing. Her car broke down during a bad storm so I brought her here. I later fixed her car and cut the downed tree blocking the road so she could get home. It wasn't a big deal, still isn't." Patch isn't the type of guy to boast. Mack leaves it at that.

"I'm sure she'll help him come to realize how wrong he is without revealing her pleasant afternoon with you. You two didn't…"

He hisses, "No, absolutely not! She's a married woman and I'll never get with another man's wife behind his back. I have absolute respect for the vows they swore to."

"I'm happy to hear that you didn't fuck my mother." I take a long swig of beer before setting the bottle on the table. "Where's Bash?"

"He's in the shower," Mack replies.

"I probably shouldn't have come here. Just say the word and I'll leave. You guys don't need to take on my bullshit."

Patch frowns. "Where else would you go? No, you'll stay here where we know you'll be safe."

"I could stay at the Presley residence. Kim is back at school so her room is available. They love me."

Mack asks, "Wasn't she your best friend in high school?" I nod. He snickers. "I nailed her on prom night."

"You didn't go to your prom," Patch says.

Startled, I ask, "You what?"

"Not my prom, hers," he corrects him. "I was getting off my shift at the mill when I saw her walking on the side of the road at night in a very fancy dress. I wasn't about to leave her alone on a highway. She said that she always thought I was sexy and didn't want to waste the opportunity. I thought maybe she was drunk, but she swore she hadn't drank anything and I couldn't smell booze on her breath. So, I pulled off the road and we spent a very memorable few hours steaming up the windows. I think about it often."

"She didn't tell me about that!" I'm shocked by her secrecy. "How did she ever keep that from me?"

"Well, maybe she thought you'd judge her harshly, like your father did to you tonight."

"I'd never judge her. I would've drilled her for details though," I say with a guilty grin and lifted brows. "I'm going to be asking her about this the next time I talk to her."

"Are you going to tell her about the past two days?" Patch asks.

"Hell no!" I gulp my beer, finishing the bottle. "Hmm, I guess I can't be upset with her for not telling me about you if I have no plans to tell her about my adventures with all of you. Maybe I'll let the past stay in the past. Perhaps one day when we're old and grey, I'll bring it up."

The bathroom door swings open followed by a cloud of steam. His eyes dart to me and immediately fill with concern. "What are you doing here?"

"I told my father that I was seeing you. He sort of kicked me out." My words are spoken with an overzealous shrug.

Mack hands me another beer and one to Bash, who is standing beside me in just a damp towel. The bulge from his unaroused cock is quite impressive. My mouth waters. I want to suck him until he's rock hard.

My pussy is sore from the fucking the three of them gave me this afternoon, but I want him to tenderly make love to me again.

"Well, you'll have to sleep in my room with me, Goldie. I hope that's all right. These hounds won't keep their paws to themselves if I don't protect you." His joking words and evil glare have everyone laughing.

"Bash, I will be honored to share your bed tonight."

Patch states, "If he doesn't keep you warm enough, you can slide in with me."

Mack quickly pipes up. "Lady, my bed is available too. I have a great tongue, as you know."

"I'm sure Bash will keep me very warm and satisfied. But thank you for your offers. I know where to find you should either need arise." Yes, I am flattered by all the attention.

We chat about our high school days and the trouble that seemed to always find them. Patch talks about a few of the sexual adventures he's had with some of the town's women but refuses to stake any names to his claims.

"I know you guys have shared women. Tell me about that," I ask. All three of them shake their heads.

Bash says, "No, those times are just for us and the ladies involved, of course. Our filthy, dirty sexual ménages will remain between us."

"But why?"

"Would you want us to tell others about our trysts with you? They might put two and two together and figure out who you are," Patch says with a raised brow.

"Never mind then. I'm no longer curious," I respond, gulping down the last few drops of my beer. "If it's okay with you guys, I'd like to take a shower. I still have all your scents on me."

"Here, I'll get you a towel," Bash says as he scurries toward the bathroom. I follow him after collecting my backpack.

I forgot to pack a nightie so Bash loans me one of his t-shirts. It just barely covers my ass but I'm grateful nonetheless. I half expect my mom to call the strangely named phone numbers listed in my contacts but she doesn't.

The night is dark and silent other than the soft snores from the beautiful man sleeping beside me. For so many years, I dreamed of being exactly where I am. I wonder if I'm going to wake up somewhere else and realize the past two days were nothing other than something incredible my lonely subconscious imagined.

I admire his lashes that seem to dance along his lids. The slope of his nose is almost perfectly straight which is odd. I remember when he broke it in grade ten. His lips are slightly parted and relaxed, allowing the deep breaths to slip freely in a soothing, rhythmic song.

His eyes pop open and look directly at me without first searching the room. It makes me uneasy. How did he know I was watching him?

"Are you okay? What's wrong?"

I smile and shake my head. "I'm fine. I couldn't sleep so I was watching you, hoping to give my brain incentive to shut down."

"Wasn't working?"

"No," I pout.

"What can I do to help you sleep?" he asks innocently enough. "Do you want something to eat?"

"No, I just want to look at you."

Bash brushes his fingers along my cheek to capture a stray tress of hair and ever so lovingly tuck it behind my ear. The gentleness in his eyes is something I'm sure few have ever seen. How lucky am I?

"You are so beautiful. What are you doing with me?" he asks.

"I was wondering the same of you."

He looks confused. "Goldie, you are the perfect woman, someone I thought should never given me a moment of her time. You're beautiful, smart, driven, strong and sexier than anyone I've ever met. Why are you here … with me? What did I ever do right to deserve this moment with you?"

"I think we're both lucky and deserving of each other."

"If this is a dream, I don't ever want to wake from it."

I lean toward him and quietly press my lips to his. My hands cradle his cheeks as I gracefully straddle him. His cock is already thick and hard when I sit on him. I feel his hand reach beneath me, so I rise up. He aims his shaft between my folds and I slowly lower myself, enveloping his full length with merely a shudder.

Bash's hands glide along my thighs, coming to rest on my hips. I nearly melt when I lift and lower for the first time and feel his fingertips dig into me as a moan escapes his depth. My pelvis rocks on him as he lifts and lowers his hips. It isn't more than a minute before I'm on the verge of losing myself to him once again. I sit straight up so I can rock much quicker and bury him deeper inside me.

With the moonlight casting its shadows upon his face, he looks more innocent than he does in full light. Most people look more dangerous in the darkness, but not Bash. I see him for who he is. I know how fragile his heart is. If I'm not careful, I will break this man's spirit. What a tragedy that would be.

His blue eyes appear darker than the bright blue the daylight proves them to be. This man is mine for as long as I allow him to be. I own him as much as he owns me. We are one, bound by this beautiful night which only the sweetest dream could have created.

He sits up, pressing his mouth to my right nipple and sucking it between his lips. As he rolls it with his tongue, the sensation shoots from my breast straight to my clitoris. I drop my weight onto him, forcing as much of his cock inside of me as possible, and grind my pussy against his strong stomach.

Both of us are breathing heavily. We're lost in each other. His body feels hard and yet so soft. He's abrasive but smooth. Strong bodied, but he is so very fragile. I look down into his eyes only to see them watching my mouth.

"I want you," I whisper. "I want all of you."

I can't hold back any longer. My body rocks wildly as if with a mind of its own. His arms wrap around me, trying to gain some level of control but I'm uncontrollable. I hold his head against my chest, hugging him to me as my hips buck feverishly. The room spins around us as my body tenses and my orgasm shreds me.

I can't tell if his cock is twitching and swelling inside of me or if it's my pussy torturing him with a multitude of wicked spasms that have me clawing my nails into his scalp. His muffled growl proves beyond a doubt that he couldn't prevent the eruption of his pleasure. When my pussy started milking his cock, it was simply too much.

He sits beneath me, his muscles clenching and his breath repeatedly catching in his throat. His cock twitches inside of me, expelling every drop of his seed in my depths. One final heavy exhale ends his climax.

I roll off him and curl up under his arm, my face resting on his chest. We lie here quietly as we slow our breathing. With a kiss to the top of my head, I am left feeling loved.

CHAPTER NINE

A sudden brightness jolts me from my thoughts. Is it morning already? I wasn't even sleeping, or was I? I don't remember falling asleep.

I roll over, pushing my face into the pillow. His scent fills my nostrils and a smile creeps across my face. I'm in Bash Bear's bed. We made love last night. I was his and he was mine. My hand glides along the sheet in search of him but he isn't here. I want him. Starting the day in the same loving way we finished last night would be wonderful.

My thoughts veer toward my father's stubbornness and my mood begins to sour. I flop onto my back and try to remember exactly how it felt to have Bash so deep inside of me. Yes, this eases my worries. Where the hell is he anyway?

I open my eyes, frustrated that he left me without so much as a good morning kiss. My senses liven up when I smell food and hear the hushed chatter of male voices from behind the closed door. With my breath held, I try to hear what they're saying.

"I'm telling you, she's mine. That girl is mine."

"No way, brother! That girl is going places. You're meant to be here, not in a big city, and you know it."

"He's not lying. Enjoy her while you can but you know she won't stay. She's meant for bigger and better than this lazy fucking town. Let her be who she's meant to be. If you hold her back, she'll only resent you later."

"I know, but I fucking love that woman!"

"You've always loved her, even when she didn't know you existed."

"She said she's always wanted me but thought I didn't want her."

"She's just saying that so you won't feel stupid for drooling so much over her tight little ass."

I quietly open the door and lean against the frame with my arms folded over one another. "I really did like him but he seemed unapproachable, as did you all. Is that a collective attribute, or did the three of you just decide one day to start acting standoffish for the sole purpose of keeping people at a distance?"

The three of them stop dead in their tracks and look at me. It's obvious they weren't expecting me to be awake and listening in on their conversation. They seem suddenly shy, none of them choosing to respond.

I snicker as I make my way toward the coffee maker. Mack holds up an empty mug which I gladly reach for. He kisses my forehead before letting me take it from him.

He whispers, "Sorry if you heard something you probably shouldn't have. It's just brother-talk."

I pour myself a mug full of the aromatic bean juice. I'm hoping this will jumpstart my weary mind and body.

Patch asks Bash, "Can you hand me that plate?"

After handing it to him, Bash walks over to me and kisses my lips with the same tenderness I felt last night. Nothing in his eyes has changed. He adores me.

Do I love him or is this simply a burst of endorphins from a new and exciting experience that fascinates me, as new relationships do? Am I simply in love with the dangerous excitement these three men incite? If it were only he and I, would the fascination still exist? I want to believe it would, but how can I be sure? Time will tell.

"You should have woken me," I whisper.

"But you were sleeping so soundly."

"You still should have woken me," I say as I attempt to walk past Patch. He wraps his huge hand around my forearm, pulling me closer to him.

With his face inches from mine, Patch's dangerous brown eyes burn hot. He hisses in a chest quivering tone, "Sit down, young one. You're our guest and will sit that pretty little ass of yours at the table while we feed you."

My pussy twitches when the grip of his hot hand eases and trails down my bare arm. I nearly melt from the tender caress. He's a brutish man that stirs my animalistic urges like no other man ever has. Bash doesn't scare me while thrilling me as much as this man-beast seems to do so easily, but it's purely a physical reaction as my heart belongs elsewhere.

I shiver when my hot ass touches the cold wooden chair. I can feel the dampness building between the folds of my pussy. As tired as I am, my body still craves Patch's ability to fuck me with a fierceness that turns me inside out.

The best distraction from my desirous thoughts is the liquid gold in the cup I'm clutching so lovingly in my hands. I cannot wait to get this fuel into my body. Morning coffee is a habit I got into when I moved into the dorm. The late nights and early mornings beckoned for caffeine. One day I'll break the habit, but today is not that day.

Mack and Bash have begun eating before Patch even sits down. He finishes cooking the last pancake and flops it on his plate before setting the pan back on the stove. I quietly eat while watching the three of them interact as if I'm not in the room. The love between these brothers is so deep that it has me wondering what it would be like to have a sibling.

When my parents have passed on, who will be my family if I'm not yet married with children of my own? They're lucky to have one another.

"What are you thinking?" Mack asks while tapping my arm.

I'm suddenly aware that all three of them are staring at me. "What?"

"You seem lost in thought. I was wondering what you're thinking?" he repeats.

"Oh, um … I was just observing how you three interact. It's foreign to me … having siblings, I mean. So, what are all of your plans for the day?"

Mack replies, "Patch has to go to work and I have to work on the plans for the new cabin I've been hired to build for a couple who currently reside in China."

"China? Why'd they buy property here of all places?"

He shrugs. "They claim it's quieter here and that's what they want."

"It seems like a long way to travel for vacation."

"They plan to retire here in about five years. In my experience, no matter the great intentions, they never stay. I build it, they come a few times and then sell after they realize their family will never take the time out of their daily lives to travel this far for a week-long visit. It's a pity really. They spend so much time and money to make the home to their exact specifications, but don't get to enjoy it as they'd hoped to."

"That is sad," I whisper while seeing the similarities of that scenario to my father's recent behavior.

"What about you, Bash? What are your plans?"

"I have a bit of work to do on the computer and then I have to go to town, but otherwise I'm all yours. What would you like to do today?"

I reply sarcastically, "I'd like for my father to come to his senses but that's not likely to happen, so I suppose my day is wide open."

"Will you come to town with me?"

"You want to be seen with me?"

He bows his head slightly and places his hand over his heart. "I would be honored to have you next to me for the whole world to see."

Mack and Patch start making cooing and kissy noises to tease him for his tender-heartedness. I laugh at their silliness. I can picture them as young boys doing exactly the same thing if one had mentioned a cute girl in his class he had a crush on. I can almost see their mother telling them, "Stop that!"

I wish I knew them better when their parents were still alive. These boys must have driven them crazy at times. I can't imagine raising three boys, each one different from the other but just as wildly spirited. What a challenge that would be.

"My father won't like it when he hears about it from nosy onlookers who don't know how to mind their own damn business."

While wearing a confused expression, he asks, "He knows you're with me, right?"

"Yes, but he won't like that I'm letting everyone in town know. He'll think I'm doing it purposely to rub it in his face. It'll make him angrier. I'm sure of it."

"You don't have to come with. If you're not ready, I understand," Bash sympathizes.

"I'll think about it, okay?" Bash nods while forcing a smile. I don't want him to think I'm ashamed to be with him because I'm not willing to shout it to the whole town. I should've said I would go and proudly wear him on my arm. But I fear my father will permanently shun me if I don't give him time to accept my decision to be with Bash before announcing it to everyone.

I quickly say, "I want to come with you."

"Are you sure? You don't have to."

"Yes, I'm sure. I want everyone to know I'm with you and that I'm not ashamed to be with you. That didn't sound right, did it? I just ... I want people to know that I trust you and that you guys are good men. People love to spread gossip, so, like the song says, let's give them something to talk about."

"Okay," he replies with a solid nod. "Should we make out in the center aisle at Baneck's Drug Mart? Better yet, we could fuck in the car in the hardware store parking lot."

"Um, no! I don't mean a nasty rumor." I shake my head and roll my eyes. "You're hopeless!"

Bash leans toward me and says, "But you want me."

I swallow and clear my throat. "I do."

With a tender kiss to my forehead, he says, "Then it's settled, you'll come to town with me."

It's quiet for a moment while everyone shoves pancakes and strawberries in their mouths. They are not delicate eaters. They can shove half of a pancake in their mouths and still close their lips to chew, but their cheeks are puffed out like chipmunks collecting nuts. I take smaller bites and try not to burst out in laughter. Had their mother been around, she would've broken them of their bad habits.

Patch says, "I think you should go home and try to talk to your parents at some point today."

The three of us stop chewing and look at him. He's right; I should, but I really don't want to. My eyes meet his expression of conviction. He wants me to settle this issue with my parents.

"It's not that I don't want you here. You're welcome to move in if you'd like. But I think you need to make peace with your family. After that, come back here and spend the night with me." His expression shows purely wicked intentions.

"Uh, she'll be staying in my room, but nice try!" Bash announces.

"As interesting as that sounds, I'll be spending my sleepover nights with Bash." My bottom lip finds its way between my teeth suggestively.

His words are spoken slowly and seductively. "You can always visit me in my bed, you know, to test its firmness. Is it too hard? No, it's just right."

My lips curl up at the edge while my eyes fixate on his. He growls, literally! He has me instantly breathing heavily, my pussy tightening and my nipples desperately trying to poke holes in my borrowed t-shirt.

"Do you want me to fuck you right now?"

I shake my head. Shit! I haven't even finished a cup of coffee yet. My body is defying me. It wants him, desperately.

"You want me, admit it," he hisses.

"If I said yes, how would you go about it?" I'm a woman playing with fire.

He sets his fork down slowly with his still eyes locked on mine. I sip my coffee delicately, hoping to bluff my way through this nerve-wracking conversation without choking on my coffee. He needs to know I can handle myself and resist him, even when my body begs otherwise.

Patch replies, "Little girl, I'd walk over to you, grab you by the arm and stand you up. I'd bend down and toss you over my shoulder and then carry you to my bed while spanking your bare ass." I swallow hard but try to appear calm. "Keep talking to me with that sassy attitude and you'll learn firsthand not to test me."

"Do you not like a woman to challenge you? Did your cock get hard when you told me what you'd like to do to me?"

"Keep it up, woman!" he threatens with eyes so dangerous, like a dog about to attack.

Mack and Bash sit back in their chairs looking from Patch to me and back, as if they're watching the most dangerous tennis match being played with a grenade. Perhaps they've never witnessed a woman taunt Patch in a battle of wills.

"I don't want to play right now," I say with conviction. "If or when I do, I'll let you know. But I'll talk to you with whatever attitude tickles my fancy and you can do nothing about it. You will not touch me against my will, I know that for a fact. So, maybe you've met your match. Back down, you won't win with me." I have no idea where this strong-willed, tough-ass woman came from, but I love her!

He leans back in his chair and takes a deep breath, letting it out very slowly. What's he thinking? I can almost see the raging inferno in his eyes. The seething dominant within him must be twitching with a need to punish me for my, what did he call it? Sassy backtalk? He's rubbing his palms together, no doubt his way of easing the need to crack my ass a dozen times while I count each one.

"I'll let you win this battle, Goldilocks, but I will have you over my knee one day soon, and you'll be begging me to spank you before I fuck you hard."

"If I ever do, you'll thank me for giving myself to you, won't you?" Who is this woman speaking out of my mouth?

His eyes twitch but as he grips the edge of the table, he calmly replies, "I'll be honored for the privilege of being allowed to touch you."

I smile proudly as if I've just won a glorious battle. I suppose I did, in a sense. Bash and Mack are still looking at him and then me, both wearing shocked expressions.

Mack says, "Hey Patch, it looks like you've met your match."

Patch glares at him but looks down at his plate, forking half of a pancake and ramming it in his mouth. Bash sits quietly chuckling to himself.

CHAPTER TEN

"Are you sure you don't want to go see your parents?" Bash asks as he turns into the parking lot of the grocery store. He pulls into a spot and shuts off the truck. "Maybe Patch is right, you should try to settle this."

"I haven't decided."

He takes my hand and lifts it to his mouth, kissing the back of it. I smile and open my door. He hops out and runs around the truck, holding the door as I step out. He puts his hand up to help me, but I opt for the assist handle instead. He shuts the door and then puts his hand out for me to take. When I only look at it, undecided whether I want to hold hands or not, he lets it drop to his side.

"It's okay if you're not ready for that yet," he says with an understanding smile.

We walk side by side through the automatic doors. They still open with the same irritating swooshing sound that hurts my ears. Bash walks over to the carts and separates one from the others. He spins it around and then quickly catches up to me. I look to him to lead the way and then follow as he makes his way toward the fresh vegetables section.

Bash doesn't seem to care at all that the middle-aged woman holding two cucumbers has her attention on us, not the vegetables. She's rudely staring with her mouth gaping.

"Goldie, how much do you want to bet she's going to take one of those cucumbers home to fuck herself? Hang on, I'll be right back."

Bash walks over to the woman. He says something to her and then proceeds to choose a cucumber from the display and examines it. He says something else to her and I watch her expression change from curiosity to shock. As he's walking back to me, he grins and waves his eyebrows.

"What did you say to her?"

"I said I was picking you a cucumber for later. And then, I said that you like the fat ones as opposed to the long, thin ones, and how you like them juicy and hard. Before I walked away, I told her I prefer to have mine thinly sliced with salt and a little cayenne, but women tend to like them for other reasons. Then, I looked at her cucumbers and told her to have a pleasant night."

"No, you didn't! Tell me you didn't!"

He's laughing.

"I did! Look, people stare at me all the time in this town. I'm sure most of them think I'm a badass who might steal their wallet if they don't watch me closely. Others, especially women, see me as a bad boy they secretly want sneaking into their bedroom to have sex with them."

"You can't possibly know what people are thinking."

"True, I'm not a psychic, but I've seen the way some women look at me and when they think I can't hear them, they say nasty shit to their friend who is also looking at me with that same expression." He tosses a bundle of apples into the cart before leaning on the handle. "Look, for some reason, people either hate us Bears or they want to have sex with us. Everyone has their perceptions, but nobody takes the time to get to know us. We may have been wild when we were young, but we've matured. So, when we get the opportunity to fuck with those who stare at us, we do. You should stop worrying about what people think of you. Odds are they're talking about you behind your back anyway. Why not give them something to talk about?"

"I can't just pretend nothing bothers me. Maybe you don't care what people think, but I do."

"Well, I think your reputation is tarnished now that you've been seen with a Bear. You might as well fall to your knees and beg their forgiveness."

"Don't be ridiculous," I hiss.

Bash shrugs and then continues pushing the cart toward the oranges. We're being watched by a teenage stock-boy, the middle-aged cashier, an older man with a cane, and Mr. Abler, the store's owner. It's creeping me out. The cucumber woman couldn't wait to get far away from us.

I hate being the reason for gossip. He's right, I shouldn't worry about what people think of me. My parents drilled it into me that I have to be pretty and well-behaved, intelligent as well as ladylike. If I didn't act accordingly, I was given a very long talking to that bored me to tears. To avoid it, I learned how to behave properly in public.

We finish food shopping and drive down the street to the drug store. Again, he attempts to assist me as I'm getting out of the truck.

"Look, you don't have to run around the truck to open the door for me or take my hand to ensure I don't fall. I'm quite capable of doing these things for myself. I appreciate that you're a gentleman, but it really isn't necessary."

Too matter-of-factly for me to argue with him, he states, "I was raised to be a gentleman and I'm not about to change now. You'll just have to get used to it."

He opens the heavy glass door and waves his hand for me to take the lead. I enter the family owned drug store, the only one in town. Bash follows me in and walks down the first aisle in search of something without a care in the world. I'm busy looking around to see if anyone is watching.

The owner, Mr. Baneck, is a pharmacist and his wife does everything else, including passing along gossip regardless of the content of which may be false rumor. She has a talent for embellishing stories until they resemble only a shadow of the truth.

They have twin daughters which are about the same age as Patch. It's rumored that one of them partied with Patch one night and ended up in his bed, but it's never been confirmed nor denied by either person. The townsfolk like to believe the girls are innocent and polished young ladies who would never have given away their virginity before marriage, especially to a vulgar, no-good, piece of shit like Patch. They were actually quite slutty but pulled the wool over everyone's eyes. I hate how most people in small towns are so incredibly naïve and judgmental.

I notice Mrs. Baneck at the counter writing something in a book. She glances up casually but quickly takes a sharp notice of Bash. Her eyes follow him as he walks down the aisle. The look on her face is one of disgust. I can't believe it. Maybe I am naïve. Did I really not notice how people look at Bash? If they only took the time to have a real conversation with him, they'd know he is an intelligent, well-spoken man who has had more education than most of them. People are assholes!

I walk up to her with a smile that could light up a room. "Hello, Mrs. Baneck. How are you this morning?"

"Oh, hello dear. I'm just fine. When do you leave to go back to school?"

"Soon. A few days," I say before looking toward Bash.

"You'd be wise to keep your distance from that boy. He's trouble," she warns.

I'm so disappointed in her. I smile again and ask, "Mrs. Baneck, do you think I'm a smart woman?"

"Yes, of course you are."

"So, you think I'm wise enough to make smart choices for myself and not be easily swindled by a snake."

"Yes, dear. What is this about?"

"If I said it looked like rain will be rolling in soon, would you go to the window to take a look for yourself or would you trust my assessment?"

She sighs heavily. "I would trust your assessment."

"Hmm," I nod thoughtfully.

Without another word, I walk right up to Bash and throw my arms over his shoulders, planting my lips on his for a very lengthy, romantic kiss. The woman gasps so loudly I fear she might be having a stroke.

He wraps his arms around my waist, holding me against him. He didn't even hesitate to kiss me back. How shallow am I to have been so concerned that people would judge me for being with him. He's more honest and worthy of my affection than anyone in this damn town, or the ten towns surrounding it. Damn her for judging him!

"Oh my god!"

Bash pulls his lips from mine and we both turn to see who said that. Mindy, the oldest of the twins, is staring at us with a shocked expression.

I've had enough of being nice. "Really Mindy? Have you forgotten who you gave your virginity to?"

"Pfft!" she scoffs, glancing nervously at her mother. "My husband on our honeymoon."

Bash corrects her. "Wrong! You might have everyone else fooled, but I know you begged my brother Patch to make you a woman when you two were in your senior year of high school. If I'm not mistaken, it happened after Vinny Lexor's beach party."

Her eyes open wide, confirming his statement without saying a word. She looks again at her mother, whose mouth is gaping. Mindy's skinny finger points at Bash as if she's going to shoot electricity from it if she can only purse her lips hard enough.

Bash takes my hand and walks up to Mrs. Baneck, dropping a box of condoms on the counter in front of her. For a split second, I'm horrified. I had no idea what he came into the store for. Now she's going to know we're having a sexual relationship. I have no doubt that she's going to call my father the instant we leave the store. Without hesitation, the rest of the town gossipers will get their ears full as well. I'm quiet on the drive out of town. Bash is kind enough not to disrupt my thoughts. I appreciate his patience.

"Can I ask what that was all about?"

I shrug. "I had enough. She was nice to me but so rude when it came to you. I didn't want her to think it was okay to talk about you like that when she so obviously doesn't know you."

He sighs. "I'm used to it. You don't have to defend me. They mean nothing to me. Therefore, their opinions and judgments are irrelevant. But I appreciate your concerns for my honor."

"Will you take me to see my parents?"

He looks over at me as if to ask if I'm sure. I nod and he smiles nervously. The remainder of the drive is spent in silence, lost in our own thoughts. No doubt he's wondering whether my father is going to chase him away with a shotgun. I keep running conversations over in my head, trying to decide how I should start the dialogue once we get there. If I tell him to have a conversation with Bash before passing judgment, maybe that'll be best. Perhaps I should tell him he's being a fool just like the ignorant people in town. Maybe not.

When we pull up and get out of the truck, I'm still not sure of what I'm going to say. Bash follows closely behind me as I make my way up the porch and up to the screen door. Before we reach it, my father slowly pushes it open and makes his way through it. I can't read what he's thinking but he isn't happy, that I'm sure of. He looks tired, as if he's aged overnight.

"Dad…" I can't find the right words, any words!

"Goldilocks, sit down," he calmly says. He looks at Bash and asks, "And you are?"

"Hello, sir. My name is Bash Bear. It's nice to finally officially meet you." Bash stands before my father with his hand extended.

My dad looks him head to toe and then reaches for his hand to briefly shake it before offering him a seat as well. They sit opposite one another. My mom leans out the door to see who is here. Her face lights up with a smile but she quickly pinches her lips together before waving at me to go in the house with her.

"I'm going to go say hi to Mom," I say softly before standing quickly and scurrying inside before either Bash or my father have a chance to protest.

Mom whispers, "Let the men talk. There's a lot they need to work through."

"Why does Dad hate him so much?"

Mom takes the jug of cold lemonade from the fridge while I line up four glasses on the counter. She begins to pour.

"Well, he doesn't hate Bash, he doesn't know Bash. You can't hate someone you don't personally know, at least, that's what your father has always said. You know, he's always saying that you might hate the actions but not necessarily the person."

"Then why did he kick me out of the house when I told him I was spending time with Bash?"

"He was upset, that's all. Your father doesn't want you to be with someone who is known to have a bad reputation. He only knows what he's heard. And that's why I asked you to come in the house. Let them have some time to talk to one another."

"Dad doesn't have his gun with him, does he?"

She jokes, "No, I hid it yesterday."

We sit at the kitchen table looking at one another. "I really like him."

"I can tell just by looking at you. Last night when your father wouldn't stop yammering on about how awful the Bear brothers are, I told him about Patch helping me during that storm."

"I'm sure that didn't go over very well."

Her eyes widen. "No, not at first. He was angry I'd kept it from him for so long. But after he calmed down, he wanted to know what Patch was really like. So, I told him that he was a perfect gentleman, very cordial. I also told him about the intelligent conversation we had while we waited for the storm to pass. I know he didn't go to college because he had to be home to raise his brothers, which is honorable. I told him that Patch said he's read at least one book a week since he was twelve years old. He loves to read because learning helps to keep his mind sharp."

She stands and takes a prepared tray of cheese and crackers from the crisper in the refrigerator. I'm not surprised. She must have cut up the cheese and laid out the crackers when my father was otherwise occupied. She knew I'd be coming home today and bringing Bash with me.

"Oh these?" she points at the tray. "I knew you'd show up at some point today. I raised you to know better than to let things stew for too long."

I look toward the door while chewing the hard skin beside my fingernail. What are they talking about? I don't hear any yelling. In fact, I don't hear anything.

Mom calmly takes my hand away from my mouth. "Don't worry, Goldilocks. They're getting along wonderfully."

"You can't possibly know that."

"If they weren't, your father would have been rushing through that door in search of his gun. Trust me, it's going to be okay. Now, grab those glasses and follow me."

I take three of them and follow Mom outside. After handing one to my Dad and one to Bash, I sit beside him while my mother sits in the lone chair closer to my father.

Dad seems calmer and Bash doesn't look as nervous as he did when we first got out of the truck. They aren't talking though and that concerns me.

"So did you two work out your issues?" Mom blurts out, cutting through the silence.

My father sighs heavily before taking a sip of his lemonade. "Well, Goldilocks, do you plan on continuing to see this man?"

"I do, yes," I reply, not liking the direction this seems to be heading in.

"And what about school?"

I clear my throat after taking a gulp from my glass. "I'm still going back in a few days. My plans for school haven't changed. I'll get my degree before I make any life-altering decisions pertaining to my future. But, as for dating Bash, I hope to continue seeing him."

"Hmm," he grumbles. After setting down his glass, he sighs again. "Bash, you seem like a decent enough young man, but I suppose time will tell that to be true or not. Your past reputation isn't a good one, but you already know that. You seem to have your head squarely on your shoulders now and you aren't afraid to work hard for what you want. In my book, that shows character. As long as Goldilocks finishes her education, I won't interfere with your relationship. If you hurt my little girl, I will not hesitate to riddle your backside with buckshot."

"I'd have it no other way," Bash replies with a smile. "Goldie is a very smart, independent, and stubborn woman. I know nothing will stop her from achieving what she sets out to do and I would never stand in her way of reaching her goals. That, sir, would be a pity."

"Bash, tell me about your brothers," Mom asks. She always knows when it's time to change the subject. She's a wise woman. I aspire to be just like her.

We sit on their porch until late in the afternoon discussing everything from childhood memories to future plans. Dad laughed hard a few times when Bash told stories about dumb things he and his brothers did as children. Some of the stories he tells us are the much more innocent versions of the terrible falsehoods the gossiping townsfolk had spun to further ruin their reputations. Bash isn't surprised to hear the false stories told about them.

CHAPTER ELEVEN

Back at the Bear residence, Mack and Patch are sitting on the sofa watching a car restoration program on television. Bash tells them how it went with my parents while I take a quick shower and slip into the same t-shirt I wore this morning at breakfast.

Bash takes a shower and meets me in his bedroom. He takes the hairdryer from me and finishes drying my hair while running his fingers through it to keep it from getting too tangled. Our eyes meet now and then in the mirror.

When his towel falls off, I reach for his lazy cock and palm it. He threatens to shut off the dryer, but I insist he finish, otherwise I'll stop touching him. The second it's dry, he shuts it off, setting it on the dresser.

In a flash, he's picked me up and tossed me onto the bed. I shriek and laugh like a high school girl on a carnival ride. We make love, our bodies moving in unison. How are we so perfectly matched, knowing how the other is going to move and moving accordingly? Maybe we were meant to be together all along.

The house is quiet and our breathing has calmed. We're lying in the darkness, entwined. His bedroom looks different as the moon casts dancing shadows from swaying trees. I feel at peace, like I belong here, like I've *always* belonged here.

Bash kisses my head then whispers, "Are you tired or do you want to have some fun?"

"We just had some fun. Didn't we?"

"Uh huh! We certainly did but I'm thinking of a different kind of fun. How would you like to slip into Patch's bed?"

"You want me to make love to your brother?"

"Not make love, no. But I want you to do what you want to do. Could you use a good hard fucking?"

"And you didn't just give me a good fucking?" I continue to tease him.

"No, Goldie. We made love, we didn't fuck. Patch fucks hard, emotionless and rather barbaric. As I recall, you really enjoyed how he fucked you over the log. If you want to sneak into his bed, I'm okay with that. Besides, it'll be a great way for you to gain some control over him."

"How do you figure?"

He snickers. "This morning he threatened that he was going to pick you up and take you to his bed. If you just go on your own and hop on him, he can't say that he took you kicking and screaming."

"He wouldn't take me if I were kicking and screaming. That would be against my will."

"Yes, but anything goes until you use your safe words."

"Uh huh, I see. You wouldn't be upset at all if I go to his bed? Like, not even the tiniest little bit?"

He looks at my face and brushes his thumb along my cheek while he cradles my face. "Goldie, I've loved you from the moment you first set your beautiful eyes on me and then smiled, making my knees weak. I'm pretty sure you love me, too. I know you're coming back to me. He won't have you forever. He and I are in no competition over your affections."

"I have a question."

"Ask me anything."

"If Patch or Mack get a girlfriend and you and I are a couple, will you go to bed with her?"

"Would that bother you?"

"If I like the woman, I don't think so. You obviously adore me." I grin conceitedly. "If I couldn't stand her, I'd have an issue. Otherwise, do as you will to her. Just remember to come home to me, okay?"

"Always! My heart will belong to you forever whether you choose to be with me or not. I've loved you from the moment I first saw you and nothing will change that." He grins. "Would you ever be with a woman?"

"I don't know. I've thought about what that would be like. How about I get used to sleeping with three men before introducing yet another new adventure?"

"There are so many adventures to be had," he says with a loving kiss on my lips. In a whisper he suggests, "Now go ride my brother."

The End of Book One

If you enjoyed the first book in The Naughty Goldie series – Goldilocks and the Three Bear Brothers, please take a moment to thank the author by leaving a review on your favourite purchasing site.
Thank you so much!

*** Continue Goldie's Story in Book 2 ***

BOOK #2
GOLDILOCKS & THE THREE BEAR BROTHERS: TRIFECTA

Sneak Peek

CHAPTER ONE

Since Bash thought it would be best for us to follow through on our educational plans before settling down together, it's been tough. Not so much my courses; it's being away from him that has me feeling lonely. Even though we talk most nights, I feel his absence when I lie in bed and don't have his hot body to snuggle up to. Neither phone nor video calls compare.

Tomorrow, I'll leave this campus for the last time. The one thing I won't miss is my lousy roommate. She is awful! Not only does she keep weird hours, but she spends most of her life on her computer and rarely showers. At first, I thought she was depressed, but she's just a weird girl.

Patch will pick me up from the airport when I touch down. No matter how much my father insisted he would be the one driving the two hours to collect me, his one and only daughter, Patch would not budge. His argument was that he sets his own working hours so it would be wiser if he made the trip rather than my father taking a day off work. I never thought I'd see my father agree with Patch Bear about anything pertaining to the bad boy spending two hours alone with me in a truck.

My clock reads 12:38 AM, two hours since I put in my earplugs and slipped an eye-mask on, hoping to block out the light flickering from my roomie's endless stream of YouTube videos. My jaw aches from clenching. I do that when I'm tense. My stomach is growling up a storm too. The apprehension about boarding a plane in the morning has me all tied up in knots. I dread flying.

Most of my belongings fit in my suitcase, which I'll be taking with me on the plane. I shipped everything else home via UPS. It's scheduled to arrive in a few days.

It's not the move back to my hometown that has me so concerned. It's telling my parents that I won't be living with them. They will not like my decision to move directly into the Bear residence where I'll be alone with Patch and Mack until Bash returns in three weeks.

Everyone in town sees the Bear brothers as being bad boys with wicked intentions. Sure, there is some truth to the rumors spread about them, but it would be wise not to listen to every nasty thing said.

My stomach tightens, and bile rises to my throat. In an instant, I'm sitting up, clutching at my chest. I rip the mask off my head and pluck the earplugs from my ear canals. Taking slow deep breaths helps.

"You okay?" Lenora looks up from behind her laptop while the bright images reflect off the lenses on her wide-framed glasses.

"Yeah, just anxiety."

"About the move?"

Yeah, idiot, about the fucking move!

"Likely." A gulp of water from the glass on my nightstand seems to push the bile back into my stomach. "I'm not moving home and haven't told my parents yet."

Intrigued at the possibility of new material for her creative writing course, she closes her computer and sets it down on the bed beside her.

"So, where will you be living?"

"My boyfriend and his two brothers live together but, as you know, Bash is away at university for a few more weeks. I'm moving into his room. I haven't told my folks yet. I don't know how they'll take that news."

She nibbles the end of her pen in a way that would likely arouse any man with a raging sexual appetite. I think I still have a ginger ale in the fridge, but the package of saltines I had for dinner is buried deep in my suitcase. Feeling the bile rising again, I dig to find them.

"Few men would ask their little brother's hot girlfriend to move in with them unless they have ulterior motives."

If she only knew! Not to let on that both of them will fuck me in every way possible many times before Bash returns home, I scoff and roll my eyes. My cheeks heat from the insinuation of her questioning leer. The discovery of the saltines calls for a quick laugh in celebration.

"Do you have a picture of them? You never showed me what they look like. I mean, your boyfriend is hot as fuck, judging by his picture on your desk, so they must be hot too, right?"

"Um..." My shoulders lift, and for a second, I wonder if showing her their picture will only urge her to question me more about my *innocent* relationship with them and if I'll be able to hide my raging sexual thoughts. "Yeah, it's the last one taken before I left to come here."

Several quick gulps of cold ginger ale urge an angry burp that I stifle. My stomach feels better in an instant. After shoving a cracker in my mouth and beginning to chew, I sit on my bed cross-legged and scroll through the vast collection of photos in search of the one I've stared at many times since we took it.

There it is: Patch, Bash, and Mack standing in a line. I'm horizontal across the screen with my mouth wide open, laughing like a fool with my blonde hair hanging in my face.

The tallest, Bash, is in the center, smiling wide while supporting my hips. The gorgeous, blue-eyed Mack hugs my calves. The only person not sporting a happy expression is Patch, who rarely smiles anyway. That's okay, it suits his persona as a mysterious, dangerous man with a lot of pent up sexual frustration. Even still, he looks unusually distant, and his normally dangerous dark-brown eyes seem softer somehow. Patch's strong arms support my shoulder and chest.

I cross the room and hand her my phone as I sit at the edge of her bed with one leg tucked beneath me.

She whistles. "Damn, girl! They are all fucking hot! How are you going to live in a house with these men and not want to fuck all of them? I wouldn't even bother wearing clothes if I were you." With her fingers on the screen, she zooms in to get a better look at them. "Shit! Can I move in too?"

Fuck no! I've had enough of her. I smile and shrug while shaking my head. She hands me my phone.

"I'd love to crash with the angry motherfucker on the end. He looks like he'd be the wildest one. I can never find a guy who's as crazy as me without him turning out to be a psychotic asshole."

Laughter escapes me, not at her comment but at a guy being crazier than her. Is it even possible?

"Patch." My fingers stretch the screen so I can see his face better. "His name is Patch. He's not crazy, just has a lot on his plate. When their parents died, he took it on himself to raise his little brothers. He was still a teenager at the time, barely eighteen. Somewhere along the line, I think he forgot how to have his own life."

"Sounds rough," she says as she picks her computer up, setting it on her lap and flipping it open. That's the cue that she's done talking, but so am I. This is the longest meaningful conversation we've had in three months.

I stand and slip on my housecoat, putting my phone in the pocket, and then slide my feet into my slippers. "I'm going to go for a walk. Don't wait up!"

The door shuts behind me, and I snicker. She'll still be up when I come back. The woman almost never sleeps. It's fucking annoying! …

I hope you enjoyed this sneak peek from **Goldilocks & the Three Bear Brothers: Trifecta**, book two.

Scan to purchase:

ABOUT THE AUTHOR

Pebbles Lacasse is a contemporary romance and erotica author. She leans toward writing bad boys desiring women who didn't know they have a kinky side. However, she's also known for her women with a dominant nature, and a secret yearning to be loved. Her books and short stories often take her readers into the BDSM lifestyle while revolving around real-life issues, and there's always a happy ending. The captivating stories of romance, love, and tender moments keep her readers coming back for more.

As someone living with Porphyria, Pebbles stays indoors to avoid UV light which gives her plenty of time to write. That's not to say she doesn't love "glamping," fishing, kayaking, and swimming, she just has to do it with protective clothing. If there's something she wants to do, she'll find a way to make it happen.

Pebbles is very family oriented. She and her husband of 30+ years raised their children in southern Ontario where she was born, and remains to this day. A 150+ pounds Mastiff takes up a lot of room in their home and in their hearts. His best friends are the two rescue cats that think they rule the home. The chickens couldn't care less about the dog until he chases them when they come too close to his outdoor toys.

Discover more about Pebbles on her website
https://www.pebbleslacasse.com

Free short story with newsletter subscription:
https://bit.ly/pebbleskinkynews
or scan the QR code below:

Keep swiping for more books you may enjoy.

MORE BOOKS BY PEBBLES LACASSE

Full Novels
My Wife and Master Jake
Broken Charm
Snowman's Burden

Series
The Complete My JoeSmith Collection Boxed Set:
The Coaching Rayna Two Book Series:
The Naughty Goldie Series:
Rule Breakers: My Best Friend's Brother, Book One

Short Stories & Novellas
Little Miss Muffet
Hello, Officer
Mistress Rabbit
A Run with Charley
Carter's Mistress
Still Waters Burn Deep
Dominatrix for Hire

Anthologies
Quarantined: A Boxed Set of Pandemic Proportions – Still Waters Burn Deep

Scan for Ebook Catalogue

CONNECT WITH PEBBLES

Facebook
https://www.facebook.com/PebblesLacasseEroticRomanceWriter/

Facebook Group
www.facebook.com/groups/pebbleslacasseandfriendsgroup/

Newsletter sign-up
https://bit.ly/pebbleskinkynews

Website
https://www.pebbleslacasse.com

Instagram
https://www.instagram.com/pebbleslacasse/

Twitter
https://twitter.com/pebbleslacasse

Goodreads
http://bit.ly/Goodreads_2y5xJji

Bookbub
https://www.bookbub.com/profile/pebbles-lacasse

Youtube
https://www.youtube.com/channel/UC3Jb8ofSw0m3TFn4cMWu5dw

TikTok
https://shorturl.at/SOzO8

SUBSCRIBE TO PEBBLES' NEWSLETTER

Sign up to receive Pebbles Lacasse's newsletter and receive a free short story to welcome you. Be among the first to read teasers from the books she's writing, learn what Pebbles does to keep her busy when she isn't writing her steamy novels, discover the captivating authors she's reading, be led to books with similar genres grouped together just for readers like you, and other crazy antics.

https://bit.ly/pebbleskinkynews

JOIN PEBBLES' TEAM

Would you like to be a valued member of my **_ARC team_**? Advanced Readers receive copies of my soon-to-be published novels to read with the promise to leave reviews by the date set by Pebbles.

You'll get **my books for FREE** forever as long as you leave reviews!

Sound like a good deal?

https://forms.gle/wyq53oMdbWSG574f8